Dr. Thorndyke Investigates

by

R. Austin Freeman

"The Discovery"
(THE BLUE SEQUIN)

Contents

The Blue Sequin

Thorndyke stood looking up and down the platform with anxiety that increased as the time drew near for the departure of the train.

"This is very unfortunate," he said, reluctantly stepping into an empty smoking compartment as the guard executed a flourish with his green flag. "I am afraid we have missed our friend." He closed the door, and, as the train began to move, thrust his head out of the window.

"Now I wonder if that will be he," he continued. "If so, he has caught the train by the skin of his teeth, and is now in one of the rear compartments."

The subject of Thorndyke's speculations was Mr. Edward Stopford, of the firm of Stopford and Myers, of Portugal Street, solicitors, and his connection with us at present arose out of a telegram that had reached our chambers on the preceding evening. It was reply-paid, and ran thus:

"CAN YOU COME HERE TO-MORROW TO DIRECT DEFENCE? IMPORTANT CASE. ALL COSTS UNDERTAKEN BY US. – STOPFORD AND MYERS."

Thorndyke's reply had been in the affirmative, and early on this present morning a further telegram – evidently posted overnight – had been delivered:

"SHALL LEAVE FOR WOLDHURST BY 8.25 FROM CHARING CROSS. WILL CALL FOR YOU IF POSSIBLE. EDWARD STOPFORD."

He had not called, however, and, since he was unknown personally to us both, we could not judge whether or not he had been among the passengers on the platform.

"It is most unfortunate," Thorndyke repeated, "for it deprives us of that preliminary consideration of the case which is so invaluable." He filled his pipe thoughtfully, and, having made a fruitless inspection of the platform at London Bridge, took up the paper that he had bought at the bookstall, and began to turn over the leaves, running his eye quickly down the columns, unmindful of the journalistic baits in paragraph or article.

"It is a great disadvantage," he observed, while still glancing through the paper, "to come plump into an inquiry without preparation – to be confronted with the details before one has a chance of considering the case in general terms. For instance–"

He paused, leaving the sentence unfinished, and as I looked up inquiringly I saw that he had turned over another page, and was now reading attentively.

"This looks like our case, Jervis," he said presently, handing me the paper and indicating a paragraph at the top of the page. It was quite brief, and was headed "Terrible Murder in Kent," the account being as follows:

"A shocking crime was discovered yesterday morning at the little town of Woldhurst, which lies on the branch line from Halbury Junction. The discovery was made by a porter who was inspecting the carriages of the train which had just come in. On opening the door of a first-class compartment, he was horrified to find the body of a fashionably-dressed woman stretched upon the floor. Medical aid was immediately summoned, and on the arrival of the divisional surgeon, Dr. Morton, it was ascertained that the woman had not been dead more than a few minutes.

"The state of the corpse leaves no doubt that a murder of a most brutal kind has been perpetrated, the cause of death being a penetrating wound of the head, inflicted with some pointed

2

implement, which must have been used with terrible violence, since it has perforated the skull and entered the brain. That robbery was not the motive of the crime is made clear by the fact that an expensively fitted dressing-bag was found on the rack, and that the dead woman's jewellery, including several valuable diamond rings, was untouched. It is rumoured that an arrest has been made by the local police."

"A gruesome affair," I remarked, as I handed back the paper, "but the report does not give us much information."

"It does not," Thorndyke agreed, "and yet it gives us something to consider. Here is a perforating wound of the skull, inflicted with some pointed implement – that is, assuming that it is not a bullet wound. Now, what kind of implement would be capable of inflicting such an injury? How would such an implement be used in the confined space of a railway-carriage, and what sort of person would be in possession of such an implement? These are preliminary questions that are worth considering, and I commend them to you, together with the further problems of the possible motive – excluding robbery – and any circumstances other than murder which might account for the injury."

"The choice of suitable implements is not very great," I observed.

"It is very limited, and most of them, such as a plasterer's pick or a geological hammer, are associated with certain definite occupations. You have a notebook?"

I had, and, accepting the hint, I produced it and pursued my further reflections in silence, while my companion, with his notebook also on his knee, gazed steadily out of the window. And thus he remained, wrapped in thought, jotting down an entry now and again in his book, until the train slowed down at Halbury Junction, where we had to change on to a branch line.

As we stepped out, I noticed a well-dressed man hurrying up the platform from the rear and eagerly scanning the faces of the few passengers who had alighted. Soon he espied us, and, approaching quickly, asked, as he looked from one of us to the other:

"Dr. Thorndyke?"

"Yes," replied my colleague, adding: "And you, I presume, are Mr. Edward Stopford?"

The solicitor bowed. "This is a dreadful affair," he said, in an agitated manner. "I see you have the paper. A most shocking affair. I am immensely relieved to find you here. Nearly missed the train, and feared I should miss you."

"There appears to have been an arrest," Thorndyke began.

"Yes – my brother. Terrible business. Let us walk up the platform; our train won't start for a quarter of an hour yet."

We deposited our joint Gladstone and Thorndyke's travelling-case in an empty first-class compartment, and then, with the solicitor between us, strolled up to the unfrequented end of the platform.

"My brother's position," said Mr. Stopford, "fills me with dismay – but let me give you the facts in order, and you shall judge for yourself. This poor creature who has been murdered so brutally was a Miss Edith Grant. She was formerly an artist's model, and as such was a good deal employed by my brother, who is a painter – Harold Stopford, you know, A.R.A. now–"

"I know his work very well, and charming work it is."

"I think so, too. Well, in those days he was quite a youngster – about twenty – and he became very intimate with Miss Grant, in quite an innocent way, though not very discreet; but she was a nice respectable girl, as most English models are, and no one thought any harm. However, a good many letters passed between them, and some little presents, amongst which was a beaded chain carrying a locket, and in this he was fool enough to put his portrait and the inscription, 'Edith, from Harold.'

"Later on Miss Grant, who had a rather good voice, went on the stage, in the comic opera line, and, in consequence, her habits and associates changed somewhat; and, as Harold had meanwhile become engaged, he was naturally anxious to get his letters back, and especially to exchange the locket for some less compromising gift. The letters she eventually sent him, but refused absolutely to part with the locket.

"Now, for the last month Harold has been staying at Halbury, making sketching excursions into the surrounding country, and yesterday morning he took the train to Shinglehurst, the third station from here, and the one before Woldhurst.

"On the platform here he met Miss Grant, who had come down from London, and was going on to Worthing. They entered the branch train together, having a first-class compartment to themselves. It seems she was wearing his locket at the time, and he made another appeal to her to make an exchange, which she refused, as before. The discussion appears to have become rather heated and angry on both sides, for the guard and a porter at Munsden both noticed that they seemed to be quarrelling; but the upshot of the affair was that the lady snapped the chain, and tossed it together with the locket to my brother, and they parted quite amiably at Shinglehurst, where Harold got out. He was then carrying his full sketching kit, including a large holland umbrella, the lower joint of which is an ash staff fitted with a powerful steel spike for driving into the ground.

"It was about half-past ten when he got out at Shinglehurst; by eleven he had reached his pitch and got to work, and he painted steadily for three hours. Then he packed up his traps, and was just starting on his way back to the station, when he was met by the police and arrested.

"And now, observe the accumulation of circumstantial evidence against him. He was the last person seen in company with the murdered woman – for no one seems to have seen her after they left Munsden; he appeared to be quarrelling with her when she was last seen alive, he had a reason for possibly wishing for her death, he was provided with an implement – a spiked staff – capable of inflicting the injury which caused her death, and, when he was searched, there was found in his possession the locket and broken chain, apparently removed from her person with violence.

"Against all this is, of course, his known character – he is the gentlest and most amiable of men – and his subsequent conduct – imbecile to the last degree if he had been guilty; but, as a lawyer, I can't help seeing that appearances are almost hopelessly against him."

"We won't say 'hopelessly,'" replied Thorndyke, as we took our places in the carriage, "though I expect the police are pretty cocksure. When does the inquest open?"

"To-day at four. I have obtained an order from the coroner for you to examine the body and be present at the post-mortem."

"Do you happen to know the exact position of the wound?"

"Yes; it is a little above and behind the left ear – a horrible round hole, with a ragged cut or tear running from it to the side of the forehead."

"And how was the body lying?"

"Right along the floor, with the feet close to the off-side door."

"Was the wound on the head the only one?"

"No; there was a long cut or bruise on the right cheek – a contused wound the police surgeon called it, which he believes

6

to have been inflicted with a heavy and rather blunt weapon. I have not heard of any other wounds or bruises."

"Did anyone enter the train yesterday at Shinglehurst?" Thorndyke asked.

"No one entered the train after it left Halbury."

Thorndyke considered these statements in silence, and presently fell into a brown study, from which he roused only as the train moved out of Shinglehurst station.

"It would be about here that the murder was committed," said Mr. Stopford; "at least, between here and Woldhurst."

Thorndyke nodded rather abstractedly, being engaged at the moment in observing with great attention the objects that were visible from the windows.

"I notice," he remarked presently, "a number of chips scattered about between the rails, and some of the chair-wedges look new. Have there been any platelayers at work lately?"

"Yes," answered Stopford, "they are on the line now, I believe – at least, I saw a gang working near Woldhurst yesterday, and they are said to have set a rick on fire; I saw it smoking when I came down."

"Indeed; and this middle line of rails is, I suppose, a sort of siding?"

"Yes; they shunt the goods trains and empty trucks on to it. There are the remains of the rick – still smouldering, you see."

Thorndyke gazed absently at the blackened heap until an empty cattle-truck on the middle track hid it from view. This was succeeded by a line of goods-waggons, and these by a passenger coach, one compartment of which – a first-class – was closed up and sealed. The train now began to slow down rather suddenly, and a couple of minutes later we brought up in Woldhurst station.

It was evident that rumours of Thorndyke's advent had preceded us, for the entire staff – two porters, an inspector, and the station-master – were waiting expectantly on the platform, and the latter came forward, regardless of his dignity, to help us with our luggage.

"Do you think I could see the carriage?" Thorndyke asked the solicitor.

"Not the inside, sir," said the station-master, on being appealed to. "The police have sealed it up. You would have to ask the inspector."

"Well, I can have a look at the outside, I suppose?" said Thorndyke, and to this the station-master readily agreed, and offered to accompany us.

"What other first-class passengers were there?" Thorndyke asked.

"None, sir. There was only one first-class coach, and the deceased was the only person in it. It has given us all a dreadful turn, this affair has," he continued, as we set off up the line. "I was on the platform when the train came in. We were watching a rick that was burning up the line, and a rare blaze it made, too; and I was just saying that we should have to move the cattle-truck that was on the mid-track, because, you see, sir, the smoke and sparks were blowing across, and I thought it would frighten the poor beasts. And Mr. Felton he don't like his beasts handled roughly. He says it spoils the meat."

"No doubt he is right," said Thorndyke. "But now, tell me, do you think it is possible for any person to board or leave the train on the off-side unobserved? Could a man, for instance, enter a compartment on the off-side at one station and drop off as the train was slowing down at the next, without being seen?"

"I doubt it," replied the station-master. "Still, I wouldn't say it is impossible."

"Thank you. Oh, and there's another question. You have a gang of men at work on the line, I see. Now, do those men belong to the district?"

"No, sir; they are strangers, every one, and pretty rough diamonds some of 'em are. But I shouldn't say there was any real harm in 'em. If you was suspecting any of 'em of being mixed up in this—"

"I am not," interrupted Thorndyke rather shortly. "I suspect nobody; but I wish to get all the facts of the case at the outset."

"Naturally, sir," replied the abashed official; and we pursued our way in silence.

"Do you remember, by the way," said Thorndyke, as we approached the empty coach, "whether the off-side door of the compartment was closed and locked when the body was discovered?"

"It was closed, sir, but not locked. Why, sir, did you think -?"

"Nothing, nothing. The sealed compartment is the one, of course?"

Without waiting for a reply, he commenced his survey of the coach, while I gently restrained our two companions from shadowing him, as they were disposed to do. The off-side footboard occupied his attention specially, and when he had scrutinized minutely the part opposite the fatal compartment, he walked slowly from end to end with his eyes but a few inches from its surface, as though he was searching for something.

Near what had been the rear end he stopped, and drew from his pocket a piece of paper; then, with a moistened finger-tip he picked up from the footboard some evidently minute object, which he carefully transferred to the paper, folding the latter and placing it in his pocket-book.

He next mounted the footboard, and, having peered in through the window of the sealed compartment, produced from his pocket a small insufflator or powder-blower, with which he blew a stream of impalpable smoke-like powder on to the edges of the middle window, bestowing the closest attention on the irregular dusty patches in which it settled, and even measuring one on the jamb of the window with a pocket-rule. At length he stepped down, and, having carefully looked over the near-side footboard, announced that he had finished for the present.

As we were returning down the line, we passed a working man, who seemed to be viewing the chairs and sleepers with more than casual interest.

"That, I suppose, is one of the plate-layers?" Thorndyke suggested to the station-master.

"Yes, the foreman of the gang," was the reply.

"I'll just step back and have a word with him, if you will walk on slowly." And my colleague turned back briskly and overtook the man, with whom he remained in conversation for some minutes.

"I think I see the police inspector on the platform," remarked Thorndyke, as we approached the station.

"Yes, there he is," said our guide. "Come down to see what you are after, sir, I expect." Which was doubtless the case, although the officer professed to be there by the merest chance.

"You would like to see the weapon, sir, I suppose?" he remarked, when he had introduced himself.

"The umbrella-spike," Thorndyke corrected. "Yes, if I may. We are going to the mortuary now."

"Then you'll pass the station on the way; so, if you care to look in, I will walk up with you."

This proposition being agreed to, we all proceeded to the police-station, including the station-master, who was on the very tiptoe of curiosity.

"There you are, sir," said the inspector, unlocking his office, and ushering us in. "Don't say we haven't given every facility to the defence. There are all the effects of the accused, including the very weapon the deed was done with."

"Come, come," protested Thorndyke; "we mustn't be premature." He took the stout ash staff from the officer, and, having examined the formidable spike through a lens, drew from his pocket a steel calliper-gauge, with which he carefully measured the diameter of the spike, and the staff to which it was fixed. "And now," he said, when he had made a note of the measurements in his book, "we will look at the colour-box and the sketch. Ha! a very orderly man, your brother. Mr. Stopford. Tubes all in their places, palette-knives wiped clean, palette cleaned off and rubbed bright, brushes wiped – they ought to be washed before they stiffen – all this is very significant." He unstrapped the sketch from the blank canvas to which it was pinned, and, standing it on a chair in a good light, stepped back to look at it.

"And you tell me that that is only three hours' work!" he exclaimed, looking at the lawyer. "It is really a marvellous achievement."

"My brother is a very rapid worker," replied Stopford dejectedly.

"Yes, but this is not only amazingly rapid; it is in his very happiest vein – full of spirit and feeling. But we mustn't stay to look at it longer." He replaced the canvas on its pins, and having glanced at the locket and some other articles that lay in a drawer, thanked the inspector for his courtesy and withdrew.

"That sketch and the colour-box appear very suggestive to me," he remarked, as we walked up the street.

11

"To me also," said Stopford gloomily, "for they are under lock and key, like their owner, poor old fellow."

He sighed heavily, and we walked on in silence.

The mortuary-keeper had evidently heard of our arrival, for he was waiting at the door with the key in his hand, and, on being shown the coroner's order, unlocked the door, and we entered together; but, after a momentary glance at the ghostly, shrouded figure lying upon the slate table, Stopford turned pale and retreated, saying that he would wait for us outside with the mortuary-keeper.

As soon as the door was closed and locked on the inside, Thorndyke glanced curiously round the bare, whitewashed building. A stream of sunlight poured in through the skylight, and fell upon the silent form that lay so still under its covering-sheet, and one stray beam glanced into a corner by the door, where, on a row of pegs and a deal table, the dead woman's clothing was displayed.

"There is something unspeakably sad in these poor relics, Jervis," said Thorndyke, as we stood before them. "To me they are more tragic, more full of pathetic suggestion, than the corpse itself. See the smart, jaunty hat, and the costly skirts hanging there, so desolate and forlorn; the dainty lingerie on the table, neatly folded – by the mortuary-man's wife, I hope – the little French shoes and open-work silk stockings. How pathetically eloquent they are of harmless, womanly vanity, and the gay, careless life, snapped short in the twinkling of an eye. But we must not give way to sentiment. There is another life threatened, and it is in our keeping."

He lifted the hat from its peg, and turned it over in his hand. It was, I think, what is called a "picture-hat" – a huge, flat, shapeless mass of gauze and ribbon and feather, spangled over freely with dark-blue sequins. In one part of the brim was a ragged hole, and from this the glittering sequins dropped off in little showers when the hat was moved.

12

"This will have been worn tilted over on the left side," said Thorndyke, "judging by the general shape and the position of the hole."

"Yes," I agreed. "Like that of the Duchess of Devonshire in Gainsborough's portrait."

"Exactly."

He shook a few of the sequins into the palm of his hand, and, replacing the hat on its peg, dropped the little discs into an envelope, on which he wrote, "From the hat," and slipped it into his pocket. Then, stepping over to the table, he drew back the sheet reverently and even tenderly from the dead woman's face, and looked down at it with grave pity. It was a comely face, white as marble, serene and peaceful in expression, with half-closed eyes, and framed with a mass of brassy, yellow hair; but its beauty was marred by a long linear wound, half cut, half bruise, running down the right cheek from the eye to the chin.

"A handsome girl," Thorndyke commented – "a dark-haired blonde. What a sin to have disfigured herself so with that horrible peroxide." He smoothed the hair back from her forehead, and added: "She seems to have applied the stuff last about ten days ago. There is about a quarter of an inch of dark hair at the roots. What do you make of that wound on the cheek?"

"It looks as if she had struck some sharp angle in falling, though, as the seats are padded in first-class carriages, I don't see what she could have struck."

"No. And now let us look at the other wound. Will you note down the description?" He handed me his notebook, and I wrote down as he dictated: "A clean-punched circular hole in skull, an inch behind and above margin of left ear – diameter, an inch and seven-sixteenths; starred fracture of parietal bone; membranes perforated, and brain entered deeply; ragged scalp-wound, extending forward to margin of left orbit; fragments of gauze and sequins in edges of wound. That will do for the present. Dr. Morton will give us further details if we want them."

He pocketed his callipers and rule, drew from the bruised scalp one or two loose hairs, which he placed in the envelope with the sequins, and, having looked over the body for other wounds or bruises (of which there were none), replaced the sheet, and prepared to depart.

As we walked away from the mortuary, Thorndyke was silent and deeply thoughtful, and I gathered that he was piecing together the facts that he had acquired. At length Mr. Stopford, who had several times looked at him curiously, said:

"The post-mortem will take place at three, and it is now only half-past eleven. What would you like to do next?"

Thorndyke, who, in spite of his mental preoccupation, had been looking about him in his usual keen, attentive way, halted suddenly.

"Your reference to the post-mortem," said he, "reminds me that I forgot to put the ox-gall into my case."

"Ox-gall!" I exclaimed, endeavouring vainly to connect this substance with the technique of the pathologist. "What were you going to do with–"

But here I broke off, remembering my friend's dislike of any discussion of his methods before strangers.

"I suppose," he continued, "there would hardly be an artist's colourman in a place of this size?"

"I should think not," said Stopford. "But couldn't you got the stuff from a butcher? There's a shop just across the road."

"So there is," agreed Thorndyke, who had already observed the shop. "The gall ought, of course, to be prepared, but we can filter it ourselves – that is, if the butcher has any. We will try him, at any rate."

He crossed the road towards the shop, over which the name "Felton" appeared in gilt lettering, and, addressing himself to the proprietor, who stood at the door, introduced himself and explained his wants.

"Ox-gall?" said the butcher. "No, sir, I haven't any just now; but I am having a beast killed this afternoon, and I can let you have some then. In fact," he added, after a pause, "as the matter is of importance, I can have one killed at once if you wish it."

"That is very kind of you," said Thorndyke, "and it would greatly oblige me. Is the beast perfectly healthy?"

"They're in splendid condition, sir. I picked them out of the herd myself. But you shall see them – ay, and choose the one that you'd like killed."

"You are really very good," said Thorndyke warmly. "I will just run into the chemist's next door, and get a suitable bottle, and then I will avail myself of your exceedingly kind offer."

He hurried into the chemist's shop, from which he presently emerged, carrying a white paper parcel; and we then followed the butcher down a narrow lane by the side of his shop. It led to an enclosure containing a small pen, in which were confined three handsome steers, whose glossy, black coats contrasted in a very striking manner with their long, greyish-white, nearly straight horns.

"These are certainly very fine beasts, Mr. Felton," said Thorndyke, as we drew up beside the pen, "and in excellent condition, too."

He leaned over the pen and examined the beasts critically, especially as to their eyes and horns; then, approaching the nearest one, he raised his stick and bestowed a smart tap on the under-side of the right horn, following it by a similar tap on the left one, a proceeding that the beast viewed with stolid surprise.

15

"The state of the horns," explained Thorndyke, as he moved on to the next steer, "enables one to judge, to some extent, of the beast's health."

"Lord bless you, sir," laughed Mr. Felton, "they haven't got no feeling in their horns, else what good 'ud their horns be to 'em?"

Apparently he was right, for the second steer was as indifferent to a sounding rap on either horn as the first. Nevertheless, when Thorndyke approached the third steer, I unconsciously drew nearer to watch; and I noticed that, as the stick struck the horn, the beast drew back in evident alarm, and that when the blow was repeated, it became manifestly uneasy.

"He don't seem to like that," said the butcher. "Seems as if – Hullo, that's queer!"

Thorndyke had just brought his stick up against the left horn, and immediately the beast had winced and started back, shaking his head and moaning. There was not, however, room for him to back out of reach, and Thorndyke, by leaning into the pen, was able to inspect the sensitive horn, which he did with the closest attention, while the butcher looked on with obvious perturbation.

"You don't think there's anything wrong with this beast, sir, I hope," said he.

"I can't say without a further examination," replied Thorndyke. "It may be the horn only that is affected. If you will have it sawn off close to the head, and sent up to me at the hotel, I will look at it and tell you. And, by way of preventing any mistakes, I will mark it and cover it up, to protect it from injury in the slaughter-house."

He opened his parcel and produced from it a wide-mouthed bottle labelled "Ox-gall," a sheet of gutta-percha tissue, a roller bandage, and a stick of sealing-wax. Handing the bottle to Mr. Felton, he encased the distal half of the horn in a covering by means of the tissue and the bandage, which he fixed securely with the sealing-wax.

"I'll saw the horn off and bring it up to the hotel myself, with the ox-gall," said Mr. Felton. "You shall have them in half an hour."

He was as good as his word, for in half an hour Thorndyke was seated at a small table by the window of our private sitting-room in the Black Bull Hotel. The table was covered with newspaper, and on it lay the long grey horn and Thorndyke's travelling-case, now open and displaying a small microscope and its accessories. The butcher was seated solidly in an armchair waiting, with a half-suspicious eye on Thorndyke for the report; and I was endeavouring by cheerful talk to keep Mr. Stopford from sinking into utter despondency, though I, too, kept a furtive watch on my colleague's rather mysterious proceedings.

I saw him unwind the bandage and apply the horn to his ear, bending it slightly to and fro. I watched him, as he scanned the surface closely through a lens, and observed him as he scraped some substance from the pointed end on to a glass slide, and, having applied a drop of some reagent, began to tease out the scraping with a pair of mounted needles. Presently he placed the slide under the microscope, and, having observed it attentively for a minute or two, turned round sharply.

"Come and look at this, Jervis," said he.

I wanted no second bidding, being on tenterhooks of curiosity, but came over and applied my eye to the instrument.

"Well, what is it?" he asked.

"A multipolar nerve corpuscle – very shrivelled, but unmistakable."

"And this?"

He moved the slide to a fresh spot.

"Two pyramidal nerve corpuscles and some portions of fibres."

"And what do you say the tissue is?"

"Cortical brain substance, I should say, without a doubt."

"I entirely agree with you. And that being so," he added, turning to Mr. Stopford, "we may say that the case for the defence is practically complete."

"What, in Heaven's name, do you mean?" exclaimed Stopford, starting up.

"I mean that we can now prove when and where and how Miss Grant met her death. Come and sit down here, and I will explain. No, you needn't go away, Mr. Felton. We shall have to subpoena you. Perhaps," he continued, "we had better go over the facts and see what they suggest. And first we note the position of the body, lying with the feet close to the off-side door, showing that, when she fell, the deceased was sitting, or more probably standing, close to that door. Next there is this." He drew from his pocket a folded paper, which he opened, displaying a tiny blue disc. "It is one of the sequins with which her hat was trimmed, and I have in this envelope several more which I took from the hat itself.

"This single sequin I picked up on the rear end of the off side footboard, and its presence there makes it nearly certain that at some time Miss Grant had put her head out of the window on that side.

"The next item of evidence I obtained by dusting the margins of the off-side window with a light powder, which made visible a greasy impression three and a quarter inches long on the sharp corner of the right-hand jamb (right-hand from the inside, I mean).

"And now as to the evidence furnished by the body. The wound in the skull is behind and above the left ear, is roughly circular, and measures one inch and seven-sixteenths at most, and a ragged scalp-wound runs from it towards the left eye. On the right cheek is a linear contused wound three and a quarter inches long. There are no other injuries.

"Our next facts are furnished by this." He took up the horn and tapped it with his finger, while the solicitor and Mr. Felton stared at him in speechless wonder. "You notice it is a left horn, and you remember that it was highly sensitive. If you put your ear to it while I strain it, you will hear the grating of a fracture in the bony core. Now look at the pointed end, and you will see several deep scratches running lengthwise, and where those scratches end the diameter of the horn is, as you see by this calliper-gauge, one inch and seven-sixteenths. Covering the scratches is a dry blood-stain, and at the extreme tip is a small mass of a dried substance which Dr. Jervis and I have examined with the microscope and are satisfied is brain tissue."

"Good God!" exclaimed Stopford eagerly. "Do you mean to say–"

"Let us finish with the facts, Mr. Stopford," Thorndyke interrupted. "Now, if you look closely at that blood-stain, you will see a short piece of hair stuck to the horn, and through this lens you can make out the root-bulb. It is a golden hair, you notice, but near the root it is black, and our calliper-gauge shows us that the black portion is fourteen sixty-fourths of an inch long. Now, in this envelope are some hairs that I removed from the dead woman's head. They also are golden hairs, black at the roots, and when I measure the black portion I find it to be fourteen sixty-fourths of an inch long. Then, finally, there is this."

He turned the horn over, and pointed to a small patch of dried blood. Embedded in it was a blue sequin.

Mr. Stopford and the butcher both gazed at the horn in silent amazement; then the former drew a deep breath and looked up at Thorndyke.

19

"No doubt," said he, "you can explain this mystery, but for my part I am utterly bewildered, though you are filling me with hope."

"And yet the matter is quite simple," returned Thorndyke, "even with these few facts before us, which are only a selection from the body of evidence in our possession. But I will state my theory, and you shall judge." He rapidly sketched a rough plan on a sheet of paper, and continued: "These were the conditions when the train was approaching Woldhurst: Here was the passenger-coach, here was the burning rick, and here was a cattle-truck. This steer was in that truck. Now my hypothesis is that at that time Miss Grant was standing with her head out of the off-side window, watching the burning rick. Her wide hat, worn on the left side, hid from her view the cattle-truck which she was approaching, and then this is what happened." He sketched another plan to a larger scale. "One of the steers – this one – had thrust its long horn out through the bars. The point of that horn struck the deceased's head, driving her face violently against the corner of the window, and then, in disengaging, ploughed its way through the scalp, and suffered a fracture of its core from the violence of the wrench. This hypothesis is inherently probable, it fits all the facts, and those facts admit of no other explanation."

The solicitor sat for a moment as though dazed; then he rose impulsively and seized Thorndyke's hands. "I don't know what to say to you," he exclaimed huskily, "except that you have saved my brother's life, and for that may God reward you!"

The butcher rose from his chair with a slow grin.

"It seems to me," said he, "as if that ox-gall was what you might call a blind, eh, sir?"

And Thorndyke smiled an inscrutable smile.

When we returned to town on the following day we were a party of four, which included Mr. Harold Stopford. The verdict of "Death by misadventure," promptly returned by the coroner's jury, had been shortly followed by his release from custody, and he now sat with his brother and me, listening with rapt attention to Thorndyke's analysis of the case.

"So, you see," the latter concluded, "I had six possible theories of the cause of death worked out before I reached Halbury, and it only remained to select the one that fitted the facts. And when I had seen the cattle-truck, had picked up that sequin, had heard the description of the steers, and had seen the hat and the wounds, there was nothing left to do but the filling in of details."

"And you never doubted my innocence?" asked Harold Stopford.

Thorndyke smiled at his quondam client.

"Not after I had seen your colour-box and your sketch," said he, "to say nothing of the spike."

The New Jersey Sphinx

"A rather curious neighbourhood this, Jervis," my friend Thorndyke remarked as we turned into Upper Bedford Place; "a sort of aviary for cosmopolitan birds of passage, especially those of the Oriental variety. The Asiatic and African faces that one sees at the windows of these Bloomsbury boarding houses almost suggest an overflow from the ethnographical galleries of the adjacent British Museum."

"Yes," I agreed," there must be quite a considerable population of Africans, Japanese and Hindus in Bloomsbury; particularly Hindus."

As I spoke, and as if in illustration of my statement, a dark-skinned man rushed out of one of the houses farther down the street and began to advance towards us in a rapid, bewildered fashion, stopping to look at each street door as he came to it. His hatless condition – though he was exceedingly well dressed – and his agitated manner immediately attracted my attention, and Thorndyke's too, for the latter remarked, " Our friend seems to be in trouble. An accident, perhaps, or a case of sudden illness."

Here the stranger, observing our approach, ran for ward to meet us and asked in an agitated tone, "Can you tell me, please, where I can find a doctor?"

"I am a medical man," replied Thorndyke, "and so is my friend."

Our acquaintance grasped Thorndyke's sleeve and exclaimed eagerly, "Come with me, then, quickly, if you please. A most dreadful thing has happened."

He hurried us along at something between a trot and a quick walk, and as we proceeded he continued excitedly, "I am quite confused and terrified; it is all so strange and sudden and terrible."

"Try," said Thorndyke, "to calm yourself a little and tell us what has happened."

"I will," was the agitated reply. "It is my cousin, Dinanath Byramji – his surname is the same as mine. Just now I went to his room and was horrified to find him lying on the floor, staring at the ceiling and blowing – like this," and he puffed out his cheeks with a soft blowing noise. "I spoke to him and shook his hand, but he was like a dead man. This is the house."

He darted up the steps to an open door at which a rather scared page-boy was on guard, and running along the hall, rapidly ascended the stairs. Following him closely, we reached a rather dark first-floor landing where, at a half-open door, a servant-maid stood listening with an expression of awe to a rhythmical snoring sound that issued from the room.

The unconscious man lay as Mr. Byramji had said staring fixedly at the ceiling with wide-open, glazy eyes, puffing out his cheeks slightly at each breath. But the breathing was shallow and slow, and it grew perceptibly slower, with lengthening pauses. And even as I was timing it with my watch while Thorndyke examined the pupils with the aid of a wax match, it stopped. I laid my finger on the wrist and caught one or two slow, flickering beats. Then the pulse stopped too.

"He is gone, said I. "He must have burst one of the large arteries."

"Apparently," said Thorndyke, "though one would not have expected it at his age. But wait! What is this?"

23

He pointed to the right ear, in the hollow of which a few drops of blood had collected, and as he spoke he drew his hand gently over the dead man's head and moved it slightly from side to side.

"There is a fracture of the base of the skull," said he, "and quite distinct signs of contusion of the scalp." He turned to Mr. Byramji, who stood wringing his hand and gazing incredulously at the dead man, and asked: "Can you throw any light on this?"

The Indian looked at him vacantly. The sudden tragedy seemed to have paralysed his brain. "I don't understand," said he. "What does it mean?"

"It means," replied Thorndyke, "that he has received a heavy blow on the head."

For a few moments Mr. Byramji continued to stare vacantly at my colleague. Then he seemed suddenly to realise the import of Thorndyke's remark, for he started up excitedly and turned to the door, outside which the two servants were hovering.

"Where is the person gone who came in with my cousin?" he demanded.

"You saw him go out, Albert," said the maid. "Tell Mr. Byramji where he went to."

The page tiptoed into the room with a fearful eye fixed on the corpse, and replied falteringly, "I only see the back of him as he went out, and all I know is that he turned to the left. P'raps he's gone for a doctor."

"Can you give us any description of him?" asked Thorndyke.

"I only see the back of him," repeated the page. "He was a shortish gentleman and he had on a dark suit of clothes and a hard felt hat. That's all I know."

"Thank you," said Thorndyke. "We may want to ask you some more questions presently." and having conducted the page to the door, he shut it and turned to Mr. Byramji.

"Have you any idea who it was that was with your cousin?" he asked.

"None at all," was the reply. "I was sitting in my room opposite, writing, when I heard my cousin come up the stairs with another person, to whom he was talking. I could not hear what he was saying. They went into his room – this room – and I could occasionally catch the sound of their voices. In about a quarter of an hour I heard the door open and shut, and then someone went downstairs, softly and rather quickly. I finished the letter that I was writing, and when I had addressed it I came in here to ask my cousin who the visitor was. I thought it might be someone who had come to negotiate for the ruby."

"The ruby!" exclaimed Thorndyke. "What ruby do you refer to?"

"The great ruby," replied Byramji. "But of course you have not–" He broke off suddenly and stood for a few moments staring at Thorndyke with parted lips and wide-open eyes; then abruptly he turned, and kneeling beside the dead man he began, in a curious, caressing, half-apologetic manner, first to pass his hands gently over the body at the waist and then to unfasten the clothes. This brought into view a handsome, soft leather belt, evidently of native workmanship, worn next to the skin and furnished with three pockets. Mr. Byramji unbuttoned and explored them in quick succession, and it was evident that they were all empty.

"It is gone!" he exclaimed in low, intense tones, "Gone! Ah! But how little would it signify! But thou, dear Dinanath, my brother, my friend, thou art gone, too!"

He lifted the dead man's hand and pressed it to his cheek, murmuring endearments in his own tongue. Presently he laid it down reverently, and sprang up, and I was startled at the change in his aspect. The delicate, gentle, refined face had suddenly become the face of a Fury – fierce, sinister, vindictive.

"This wretch must die!" he exclaimed huskily. "This sordid brute who, without compunction, has crushed out a precious life as one would carelessly crush a fly, for the sake of a paltry crystal – he must die, if I have to follow him and strangle him with my own hands!"

Thorndyke laid his hand on Byramji's shoulder. "I sympathise with you most cordially," said he. "If it is as you think, and appearances suggest, that your cousin has been murdered as a mere incident of robbery, the murderer's life is forfeit, and Justice cries aloud for retribution. The fact of murder will be determined, for or against, by a proper inquiry. Meanwhile we have to ascertain who this unknown man is and what happened while he was with your cousin."

Byramji made a gesture of despair. "But the man has disappeared, and nobody has seen him! What can we do?"

"Let us look around us," plied Thorndyke, "and see if we can judge what has happened in this room. What, for instance, is this?"

He picked up from a corner near the door a small leather object, which he handed to Mr. Byramji. The Indian seized it eagerly, exclaiming: "Ah! It is the little bag in which my cousin used to carry the ruby. So he had taken it from his belt."

"It hasn't been dropped, by any chance?" I suggested.

In an instant Mr. Byramji was down on his knees, peering and groping about the floor, and Thorndyke and I joined in the search. But, as might have been expected there was no sign of the ruby, nor, indeed, of anything else, excepting a hat which I picked up from under the table.

"No," said Mr. Byramji, rising with a dejected air. "It is gone – of course it is gone, and the murderous villain–"

Here his glance fell on the hat, which I had laid on the table, and he bent forward to look at it.

"Whose hat is this?" he demanded, glancing at the chair on which Thorndyke's hat and mine had been placed.

"Is it not your cousin's?" asked Thorndyke. "No, certainly not. His hat was like mine – we bought them both together. It had a white silk lining with his initials, D. B., in gold. This has no lining and is a much older hat. It must be the murderer's hat."

"If it is," said Thorndyke, "that is a most important fact – important in two respects. Could you let us see your hat?"

"Certainly," replied Byramji, walking quickly, but with a soft tread, to the door. As he went out, shutting the door silently behind him, Thorndyke picked up the derelict hat and swiftly tried it on the head of the dead man. As far as I could judge, it appeared to fit, and this Thorndyke confirmed as he replaced it on the table.

"As you see," said he, "it is at least a practical fit, which is a fact of some significance."

Here Mr. Byramji returned with his own hat, which he placed on the table by the side of the other, and thus placed, crown uppermost, the two hats were closely similar. Both were black, hard felts of the prevalent "bowler" shape, and of good quality, and the difference in their age and state of preservation was not striking; but when Byramji turned them over and exhibited their interiors it was seen that whereas the strange hat was unlined save for the leather head-band, Byramji's had a white silk lining and bore the owner's initials in embossed gilt letters.

"What happened," said Thorndyke, when he had carefully compared the two hats, "seems fairly obvious, The two men, on entering, placed their hats crown upwards on the table. In some way – perhaps during a struggle – the visitor's hat was knocked down and rolled under the table. Then the stranger, on

27

leaving, picked up the only visible hat – almost identically similar to his own – and put it on."

"Is it not rather singular," I asked, "that he should not have noticed the different feel of a strange hat?"

"I think not," Thorndyke replied. "If he noticed anything unusual he would probably assume that he had put it on the wrong way round. Remember that he would be extremely hurried and agitated. And when once he had left the house he would not dare to take the risk of returning, though he would doubtless realise the gravity of the mistake. And now," he continued, "would you mind giving us a few particulars? You have spoken of a great ruby, which your cousin had, and which seems to be missing."

"Yes. You shall come to my room and I will tell you about it; but first let us lay my poor cousin decently on his bed."

"I think," said Thorndyke, "the body ought not to be moved until the police have seen it."

"Perhaps you are right," Byramji agreed reluctantly, "though it seems callous to leave him lying there." With a sigh he turned to the door, and Thorndyke followed, carrying the two hats.

"My cousin and I," said our host, when we were seated in his own large bed-sitting-room, "were both interested in gem-stones. I deal in all kinds of stones that are found in the East, but Dinanath dealt almost exclusively in rubies. He was a very fine judge of those beautiful gems, and he used to make periodical tours in Burma in search of uncut rubies of unusual size or quality. About four months ago he acquired at Mogok, in Upper Burma, a magnificent specimen over twenty- eight carats in weight, perfectly flawless and of the most gorgeous colour. It had been roughly cut, but my cousin was intending to have it recut unless he should receive an advantageous offer for it in the meantime."

"What would be the value of such a stone?" I asked.

"It is impossible to say. A really fine large ruby of perfect colour is far, far more valuable than the finest diamond of the same size. It is the most precious of all gems, with the possible exception of the emerald. A fine ruby of five carats is worth about three thousand pounds, but of course, the value rises out of all proportion with increasing size. Fifty thousand pounds would be a moderate price for Dinanath's ruby."

During this recital I noticed that Thorndyke, while listening attentively, was turning the stranger's hat over in his hands, narrowly scrutinising it both inside and outside. As Byramji concluded, he remarked:

"We shall have to let the police know what has happened, but, as my friend and I will be called as witnesses, I should like to examine this hat a little more closely before you hand it over to them. Could you let me have a small, hard brush? A dry nail-brush would do." Our host complied readily – in fact eagerly. Thorndyke's authoritative, purposeful manner had clearly impressed him, for he said as he handed my colleague a new nail-brush: "I thank you for your help and value it. We must not depend on the police only."

Accustomed as I was to Thorndyke's methods, his procedure was not unexpected, but Mr. Byramji watched him with breathless interest and no little surprise as, laying a sheet of notepaper on the table, he brought the hat close to it and brushed firmly but slowly, so that the dust dislodged should fall on it. As it was not a very well-kept hat, the yield was considerable, especially when the brush was drawn under the curl of the brim, and very soon the paper held quite a little heap. Then Thorndyke folded the paper into a small packet and having written "outside" on it, put it in his pocket book.

"Why do you do that? "Mr. Byramji asked. "What will the dust tell you?"

"Probably nothing," Thorndyke replied. "But this hat is our only direct clue to the identity of the man who was with your

29

cousin, and we must make the most of it. Dust, you know, is only a mass of fragments detached from surrounding objects. If the objects are unusual the dust may be quite distinctive. You could easily identify the hat of a miller or a cement worker." As he was speaking he reversed the hat and turned down the leather head-lining, whereupon a number of strips of folded paper fell down into the crown.

"Ah!" exclaimed Byramji, "perhaps we shall learn something now."

He picked out the folded slips and began eagerly to open them out, and we examined them systematically- one by one. But they were singularly disappointing and uninforming. Mostly they consisted of strips of newspaper, with one or two circulars, a leaf from a price list of gas stoves, a portion of a large envelope on which were the remains of an address which read " – n – don, W.C.," and a piece of paper evidently cut down vertically and bearing the right-hand half of some kind of list. This read:

"—el 3 oz. 5 dwts.

—eep 9½ oz."

"Can you make anything of this?" I asked, handing the paper to Thorndyke.

He looked at it reflectively, and answered, as he copied it into his notebook : "It has, at least, some character. If we consider it with the other data we should get some sort of hint from it. But these scraps of paper don't tell us much. Perhaps their most suggestive feature is their quantity and the way in which, as you have no doubt noticed, they were arranged at the sides of the hat. We had better replace them as we found them for the benefit of the police."

The nature of the suggestion to which he referred was not very obvious to me, but the presence of Mr. Byramji rendered discussion inadvisable; nor was there any opportunity, for we had hardly reconstituted the hat when we became aware of a number of persons ascending the stairs, and then we heard the sound of rather peremptory rapping at the door of the dead man's room.

Mr. Byramji opened the door and went out on to the landing, where several persons had collected, including the two servants and a constable.

"I understand," said the policeman, "that there is something wrong here. Is that so?"

"A very terrible thing has happened," replied Byramji. "But the doctors can tell you better than I can." Here he looked appealingly at Thorndyke, and we both went out and joined him.

"A gentleman – Mr. Dinanath Byramji – has met with his death under somewhat suspicious circumstances," said Thorndyke, and, glancing at the knot of naturally curious persons on the landing, he continued: "If you will come into the room where the death occurred, I will give you the facts so far as they are known to us."

With this he opened the door and entered the room with Mr. Byramji, the constable, and me. As the door opened, the bystanders craned forward and a middle- aged woman uttered a cry of horror and followed us into the room.

"This is dreadful!" she exclaimed, with a shuddering glance at the corpse. "The servants told me about it when I came in just now and I sent Albert for the police at once. But what does it mean? You don't think poor Mr. Dinanath has been murdered?"

"We had better get the facts, ma'am," said the constable, drawing out a large black notebook and laying his helmet on the table. He turned to Mr. Byramji, who had sunk into a chair and sat, the picture of grief, gazing at his dead cousin. "Would you kindly tell me what you know about how it happened?"

Byramji repeated the substance of what he had told us, and when the constable had taken down his statement,

31

Thorndyke and I gave the few medical particulars that we could furnish and handed the constable our cards. Then, having helped to lay the corpse on the bed and cover it with a sheet, we turned to take our leave.

"You have been very kind," Mr. Byramji said as he shook our hands warmly. "I am more than grateful. Perhaps I may be permitted to call on you and hear if – if you have learned anything fresh," he concluded discreetly.

"We shall be pleased to see you," Thorndyke replied, "and to give you any help that we can"; and with this we took our departure, watched inquisitively down the stairs by the boarders and the servants who still lurked in the vicinity of the chamber of death.

"If the police have no more information than we have," I remarked as we walked homeward, "they won't have much to go on."

"No," said Thorndyke. "But you must remember that this crime – as we are justified in assuming it to be – is not an isolated one. It is the fourth of practically the same kind within the last six months. I understand that the police have some kind of information respecting the presumed criminal, though it can't be worth much, seeing that no arrest has been made. But there is some new evidence this time. The exchange of hats may help the police considerably."

"In what way? What evidence does it furnish?"

"In the first place it suggests a hurried departure, which seems to connect the missing man with the crime. Then, he is wearing the dead man's hat, and though he is not likely to continue wearing it, it may be seen and furnish a clue. We know that that hat fits him fairly well and we know its size, so that we know the size of his head. Finally, we have the man's own hat."

"I don't fancy the police will get much information from that," said I.

"Probably not," he agreed. "Yet it offered one or two interesting suggestions, as you probably observed."

"It made no suggestions whatever to me," said I.

"Then," said Thorndyke, "I can only recommend you to recall our simple inspection and consider the significance of what we found."

This I had to accept as closing the discussion for the time being, and as I had to make a call at my bookseller's concerning some reports that I had left to be bound, I parted from Thorndyke at the corner of Chichester Rents and left him to pursue his way alone. My business with the bookseller took me longer than I had expected, for I had to wait while the lettering on the backs was completed, and when I arrived at our chambers in King's Bench Walk, I found Thorndyke apparently at the final stage of some experiment evidently connected with our late adventure. The microscope stood on the table with one slide on the stage and a second one beside it; but Thorndyke had apparently finished his microscopical researches, for as I entered he held in his hand a test-tube filled with a smoky-coloured fluid.

"I see that you have been examining the dust from the hat," said I. "Does it throw any fresh light on the case?"

"Very little," he replied. "It is just common dust – assorted fibres and miscellaneous organic and mineral particles. But there are a couple of hairs from the in side of the hat – both lightish brown, and one of the atrophic, note-of-exclamation type that one finds at the margin of bald patches; and the outside dust shows minute traces of lead, apparently in the form of oxide. What do you make of that?"

"Perhaps the man is a plumber or a painter," I suggested.

"Either is possible and worth considering," he replied ; but his tone made clear to me that this was not his own inference; and a row of five consecutive Post Office Directories, which I had already noticed ranged along the end of the table, told me that he had not only formed a hypothesis on the subject, but had probably either confirmed or disproved it. For the Post Office Directory was one of Thorndyke's favourite books of reference; and the amount of curious and recondite information that he succeeded in extracting from its matter-of-fact pages would have surprised no one more than it would the compilers of the work.

At this moment the sound of footsteps ascending our stairs became audible. It was late for business callers, but we were not unaccustomed to late visitors; and a familiar rat-tat of our little brass knocker seemed to explain the untimely visit.

"That sounds like Superintendent Miller's knock," said Thorndyke, as he strode across the room to open the door. And the superintendent it turned out to be. But not alone.

As the door opened the officer entered with two gentlemen, both natives of India, and one of whom was our friend Mr. Byramji.

"Perhaps," said Miller," I had better look in a little later."

"Not on my account," said Byramji. "I have only a few words to say and there is nothing secret about my business. May I introduce my kinsman, Mr. Khambata, a student of the Inner Temple?"

Byramji's companion bowed ceremoniously. "Byramji came to my chambers just now," he explained, "to consult me about this dreadful affair, and he chanced to show me your card. He had not heard of you, but supposed you to be an ordinary medical practitioner. He did not realise that he had entertained an angel unawares. But I, who knew of your great reputation, advised him to put his affairs in your hands – without prejudice to the official investigations," Mr. Khambata added hastily, bowing to the superintendent.

"And I," said Mr. Byramji, "instantly decided to act on my kinsman's advice. I have come to beg you to leave no stone unturned to secure the punishment of my cousin's murderer.

34

Spare no expense. I am a rich man and my poor cousin's property will come to me. As to the ruby, recover it if you can, but it is of no consequence. Vengeance – justice is what I seek. Deliver the wretch into my hands, or into the hands of justice, and I give you the ruby or its value, freely – gladly."

"There is no need," said Thorndyke, "of such extraordinary inducement. If you wish me to investigate this case, I will do so and will use every means at my disposal, without prejudice, as your friend says, to the proper claims of the officers of the law. But you under stand that I can make no promises. I cannot guarantee success."

"We understand that," said Mr. Khambata. "But we know that if you undertake the case, everything that is possible will be done. And now we must leave you to your consultation."

As soon as our clients had gone, Miller rose from his chair with his hand in his breast pocket. "I dare say, doctor," said he, "you can guess what I have come about. I was sent for to look into this Byramji case and I heard from Mr. Byramji that you had been there and that you had made a minute examination of the missing man's hat. So have I; and I don't mind telling you that I could learn nothing from it."

"I haven't learnt much myself," said Thorndyke.

"But you've picked up something," urged Miller, "if it is only a hint; and we have just a little clue. There is very small doubt that this is the same man – 'The New Jersey Sphinx,' as the papers call him – that committed those other robberies; and a very difficult type of criminal he is to get hold of. He is bold, he is wary, he plays a lone hand, and he sticks at nothing. He has no confederates, and he kills every time. The American police never got near him but once; and that once gives us the only clues we have."

"Finger-prints?" inquired Thorndyke.

"Yes, and very poor ones, too. So rough that you can hardly make out the pattern. And even those are not absolutely guaranteed to be his; but in any case, finger-prints are not much use until you've got the man. And there is a photograph of the fellow himself, But it is only a snapshot, and a poor one at that. All it shows is that he has a mop of hair and a pointed beard – or at least he had when the photograph was taken. But for identification purposes it is practically worthless. Still, there it is; and what I propose is this: we want this man and so do you; we've worked together before and can trust one another. I am going to lay my cards on the table and ask you to do the same."

"But, my dear Miller," said Thorndyke, "I haven't any cards. I haven't a single solid fact."

The detective was visibly disappointed. Nevertheless, he laid two photographs on the table and pushed them towards Thorndyke, who inspected them through his lens and passed them to me.

"The pattern is very indistinct and broken up," he remarked.

"Yes," said Miller; "the prints must have been made on a very rough surface, though you get prints something like those from fitters or other men who use files and handle rough metal. And now, doctor, can't you give us a lead of any kind?"

Thorndyke reflected a few moments. "I really have not a single real fact," said he, "and I am unwilling to make merely speculative suggestions."

"Oh, that's all right," Miller replied cheerfully. "Give us a start. I shan't complain if it comes to nothing."

"Well," Thorndyke said reluctantly, "I was thinking of getting a few particulars as to the various tenants of No. 51 Clifford's Inn. Perhaps you could do it more easily and it might be worth your while."

"Good!" Miller exclaimed gleefully. "He 'gives to airy nothing a local habitation and a name.'"

"It is probably the wrong name," Thorndyke reminded him.

"I don't care," said Miller. "But why shouldn't we go together? It's too late to-night, and I can't manage to-morrow morning. But say to-morrow after noon. Two heads are better than one, you know, especially when the second one is yours. Or perhaps," he added, with a glance at me, "three would be better still."

Thorndyke considered for a moment or two and then looked at me.

"What do you say, Jervis?" he asked.

As my afternoon was unoccupied, I agreed with enthusiasm, being as curious as the superintendent to know how Thorndyke had connected this particular locality with the vanished criminal, and Miller departed in high spirits with an appointment for the morrow three o'clock in the afternoon.

For some time after the superintendent's depart I sat wrapped in profound meditation. In some mysterious way the address, 51 Clifford's Inn, had emerged from the formless data yielded by the derelict hat. But what had been the connection? Apparently the fragment of the addressed envelope had furnished the clue. But how had Thorndyke extended " – n" into "51, Clifford's Inn"? It was to me a complete mystery.

Meanwhile, Thorndyke had seated himself at writing-table, and I noticed that of the two letters which he wrote, one was written on our headed paper and other on ordinary plain notepaper. I was speculating on the reason for this when he rose, and as he stuck on the stamps, said to me, "I am just going out to post these two letters. Do you care for a short stroll through the leafy shades of Fleet Street? The evening is still young."

"The rural solitudes of Fleet Street attract me I all hours," I replied, fetching my hat from the adjoining office, and we accordingly sallied forth together, strolling up King's Bench Walk and emerging into Fleet Street by way of Mitre Court.

When Thorndyke had dropped his letters into the post office box he stood awhile gazing up at the tower of St. Dunstan's Church."

"Have you ever been in Clifford's Inn, Jervis?" he inquired.

"Never," I replied (we passed through it together on an average a dozen times a week), "but it is not too late for an exploratory visit."

We crossed the road, and entering Clifford's Inn Passage, passed through the still half-open gate, crossed the outer court and threaded the tunnel-like entry by the hall to the inner court, in the middle of which Thorndyke halted, and looking up at one of the ancient houses, remarked, "No. 51."

"So that is where our friend hangs out his flag," said I.

"Oh come, Jervis," he protested, "I am surprised at you; you are as bad as Miller. I have merely suggested a possible connection between these premises and the hat that was left at Bedford Place. As to the nature of that connection I have no idea, and there may be no connection at all. I assure you, Jervis, that I am on the thinnest possible ice. I am working on a hypo thesis which is in the highest degree speculative, and I should not have given Miller a hint but that he was so eager and so willing to help – and also that I wanted his finger-prints. But we are really only at the beginning, and may never get any farther."

I looked up at the old house. It was all in darkness excepting the top floor, where a couple of lighted windows showed the shadow of a man moving rapidly about the room. We crossed to the entry and inspected the names painted on the door-posts. The ground floor was occupied by a firm of photo-engravers, the first floor by a Mr. Carrington, whose name stood out conspicuously on its oblong of comparatively fresh white paint, while the tenants of the second floor – old residents, to judge by the faded and discoloured paint in which their names were announced – were Messrs. Burt & Highley, metallurgists.

"Burt has departed," said Thorndyke, as I read out the names; and he pointed to two red lines of erasure which I had not noticed in the dim light, "so the active gentleman above is presumably Mr. Highley, and we may take it that he has residential as well as business premises. I wonder who and what Mr. Carrington is – but I dare say we shall find out to-morrow."

With this he dismissed the professional aspects of Clifford's Inn, and, changing the subject to its history and associations, chatted in his inimitable, picturesque manner until our leisurely perambulations brought us at length to the Inner Temple Gate.

On the following morning we bustled through our work in order to leave the afternoon free, making several joint visits to solicitors from whom we were taking instructions. Returning from the last of these – a City lawyer – Thorndyke turned into St. Helen's Place and halted at a doorway bearing the brass plate of a firm of assayists and refiners. I followed him into the outer office, where, on his mentioning his name, an elderly man came to the counter.

"Mr. Grayson has put out some specimens for you, sir," said he. "They are about thirty grains to the ton – you said that the content was of no importance – I am to tell you that you need not return them. They are not worth treating." He went to a large safe from which he took a canvas bag, and returning to the counter, turned out on it the contents of the bag, consisting , about a dozen good-sized lumps of quartz and a glittering yellow fragment, which Thorndyke picked out and dropped in his pockct.

"Will that collection do?" our friend inquired.

"It will answer my purpose perfectly," Thorndyke replied, and when the specimens had been replaced the bag, and the latter deposited in Thorndyke's hand-bag, my colleague thanked the assistant and we went on our way.

"We extend our activities into the domain of mineralogy," I remarked.

Thorndyke smiled an inscrutable smile. "We also employ the suction pump as an instrument of research," he observed. "However, the strategic uses of chunks of quartz – otherwise than as missiles – will develop themselves in due course, and the interval may be used for reflection."

It was. But my reflection brought no solution. I noticed, however, that when at three o'clock we set forth in company with the superintendent, the bag went with us; and having offered to carry it and having had my offer accepted with a sly twinkle, its weight assured me that the quartz was still inside.

"Chambers and Offices to let," Thorndyke read aloud as we approached the porter's lodge. "That lets us in, I think. And the porter knows Dr. Jervis and me by sight, so he will talk more freely."

"He doesn't know me," said the superintendent, "but I'll keep in the background, all the same."

A pull at the bell brought out a clerical-looking man in a tall hat and a frock coat, who regarded Thorndyke and me through his spectacles with an amiable air of recognition.

"Good afternoon, Mr. Larkin," said Thorndyke. "I am asked to get particulars of vacant chambers. What have you got to let?

Mr. Larkin reflected. "Let me see. There's a ground floor at No. 5 – rather dark – and a small second- pair set at No. 12. And then there is – oh, yes, there is a good first-floor set at No. 51. They wouldn't have been vacant until Michaelmas, but Mr. Carrington, the tenant, has had to go abroad suddenly. I had a letter from him this morning, enclosing the key. Funny letter, too." He dived into his pocket, and hauling out a bundle of letters, selected one and handed it to Thorndyke with a broad smile.

Thorndyke glanced at the postmark ("London, E."), and having taken out the key, extracted the letter, which he opened and held so that Miller and I could see it. The paper bore the printed heading, "Baltic Shipping Company, Wapping," and the further written heading, "S.S. Gothenburg," and the letter was brief and to the point:

DEAR SIR,

I am giving up my chambers at No. 51, as I have been suddenly called abroad. I enclose the key, but am not troubling you with the rent. The sale of my costly furniture will more than cover it, and the surplus can be expended on painting the garden railings,

Yours sincerely,

A. CARRINGTON.

Thorndyke smilingly replaced the letter and the key in the envelope and asked: "What is the furniture like?"

"You'll see," chuckled the porter, "if you care to look at the rooms. And I think they might suit, They're a good set."

"Quiet?"

""Yes, pretty quiet. There's a metallurgist overhead – Highley – used to be Burt & Highley, but Burt has gone to the City, and I don't think Highley does much business now."

"Let me see," said Thorndyke, "I think I used to meet Highley sometimes – a tall, dark man, isn't he?"

"No, that would be Burt. Highley is a little, fairish man, rather bald, with a pretty rich complexion" – here Mr. Larkin tapped his nose knowingly and raised his little finger – "which may account for the falling off of business."

"Hadn't we better have a look at the rooms?" Miller interrupted a little impatiently.

"Can we see them, Mr. Larkin?" asked Thorndyke.

"Certainly," was the reply. "You've got the key. Let me have it when you've seen the rooms; and whatever ever you do," he added with a broad grin, "be careful of the furniture."

"It looks," the superintendent remarked as we crossed the inner court, "as if Mr. Carrington had done a mizzle. That's hopeful. And I see," he continued, glancing at the fresh paint on the door-post as we passed through the entry, "that he hasn't been here long. That's hopeful, too."

We ascended to the first floor, and as Thorndyke unlocked and threw open the door, Miller laughed aloud. The "costly furniture" consisted of a small kitchen table, a Windsor chair and a dilapidated deck- chair. The kitchen contained a gas ring, a small saucepan and a frying-pan, and the bedroom was furnished with a camp-bed devoid of bed-clothes, a wash-hand basin on a packing-case, and a water can.

"Hallo!" exclaimed the superintendent. "He's left a hat behind. Quite a good hat, too." He took it down from the peg, glanced at its exterior and then, turning it over, looked inside. And then his mouth opened with a jerk.

"Great Solomon Eagle!" he gasped. "Do you see, doctor? It's THE hat."

He held it out to us, and sure enough on the white silk lining of the crown were the embossed, gilt letters, D.B., just as Mr. Byramji had described them.

"Yes," Thorndyke agreed, as the superintendent snatched up a greengrocer's paper bag from the kitchen floor and persuaded the hat into it, "it is undoubtedly the missing link. But what are you going to do now?"

"Do!" exclaimed Miller. "Why, I am going to collar the man. These Baltic boats put in at Hull and Newcastle – perhaps he didn't know that – and they are pretty slow boats, too. I shall wire to Newcastle to have the ship detained and take Inspector

Badger down to make the arrest. I'll leave you to explain to the porter, and I owe you a thousand thanks for your valuable tip."

With this he bustled away, clasping the precious hat and from the window we saw him hurry across the court and dart out through the postern into Fetter Lane.

"I think Miller was rather precipitate," said Thorndyke. "He should have got a description of the man and some further particulars."

"Yes," said I. "Miller had much better have waited until you had finished with Mr. Larkin. But you can get some more particulars when we take back the key."

"We shall get more information from the gentleman who lives on the floor above, and I think we will go up and interview him now. I wrote to him last night and made a metallurgical appointment, signing myself W. Polton. Your name, if he should ask, is Stevenson."

As we ascended the stairs to the next floor, I meditated on the rather tortuous proceedings of my usually straightforward colleague. The use of the lumps of quartz was now obvious; but why these mysterious tactics? And why, before knocking at the door, did Thorndyke carefully take the reading of the gas meter on the landing?

The door was opened in response to our knock – a shortish, alert-looking, clean-shaved man in a white overall, who looked at us keenly and rather forbiddingly. But Thorndyke was geniality personified.

"How do you do, Mr. Highley?" said he, holding out his hand, which the metallurgist shook coolly. "You got my letter, I suppose?"

"Yes. But I am not Mr. Highley. He's away and I am carrying on. I think of taking over his business if there is any to take over. My name is Sherwood. Have you got the samples?"

Thorndyke produced the canvas bag, which Mr. Sherwood took from him and emptied out on a bench, picking up the lumps of quartz one by one and examining them closely. Meanwhile Thorndyke took a rapid survey of the premises. Against the wall were two cupel furnaces and a third larger furnace like a small pottery kiln. On a set of narrow shelves were several rows of bone-ash cupels, looking like little white flower-pots, and near them was the cupel-press – an appliance into which powdered bone-ash was fed and compressed by a plunger to form the cupels – while by the side of the press was a tub of bone-ash – a good deal coarser, I noticed, than the usual fine powder. This coarseness was also observed by Thorndyke, who edged up to the tub and dipped his hand into the ash and then wiped his fingers on his handkerchief.

"This stuff doesn't seem to contain much gold," said Mr. Sherwood. "But we shall see when we make the assay."

"What do you think of this?" asked Thorndyke, taking from his pocket the small lump of glittering, golden-looking mineral that he had picked out at the assayist's. Mr. Sherwood took it from him and examined it closely. "This looks more hopeful," said he; "rather rich, in fact."

Thorndyke received this statement with an unmoved countenance; but as for me, I stared at Mr. Sherwood in amazement. For this lump of glittering mineral was simply a fragment of common iron pyrites! It would not have deceived a schoolboy, much less a metallurgist.

Still holding the specimen, and taking a watchmaker's lens from a shelf, Mr. Sherwood moved over to the window. Simultaneously, Thorndyke stepped softly to the cupel shelves and quickly ran his eye along the rows of cupels. Presently he paused at one, examined it more closely, and then, taking it from the shelf, began to pick at it with his finger-nail.

At this moment Mr. Sherwood turned and observed him; and instantly there flashed into the metallurgist's face an expression of mingled anger and alarm.

"Put that down!" he commanded peremptorily, and then, as Thorndyke continued to scrape with his finger nail, he shouted furiously, "Do you hear? Drop it!"

Thorndyke took him literally at his word and let the cupel fall on the floor, when it shattered into innumerable fragments, of which one of the largest separated itself from the rest. Thorndyke pounced upon it, and in an instantaneous glance, as he picked it up, I recognised it as a calcined tooth.

Then followed a few moments of weird, dramatic silence. Thorndyke, holding the tooth between his finger and thumb, looked steadily into the eyes of the metallurgist; and the latter, pallid as a corpse, glared at Thorndyke and furtively unbuttoned his overall.

Suddenly the silence broke into a tumult as bewildering as the crash of a railway collision. Sherwood's right hand darted under his overall. Instantly, Thorndyke snatched up another cupel and hurled it with such truth of aim that it shattered on the metallurgist's forehead. And as he flung the missile, he sprang forward, and delivered a swift upper-cut. There was a thunderous crash, a cloud of white dust, and an automatic pistol clattered along the floor.

I snatched up the pistol and rushed to my friend's assistance. But there was no need. With his great strength and his uncanny skill – to say nothing of the effects of the knock-out blow – Thorndyke had the man pinned down immovably.

"See if you can find some cord, Jervis," he said a calm, quiet tone that seemed almost ridiculously out of character with the circumstances.

There was no difficulty about this, for several corded boxes stood in a corner of the laboratory. I cut off two lengths, with one of which I secured the prostrate man's arms. and with the other fastened his knees and ankles.

"Now," said Thorndyke, "if you will take charge of his hands, we will make a preliminary inspection. Let us first see if he wears a belt."

Unbuttoning the man's waistcoat, he drew up the shirt, disclosing a broad, webbing belt furnished with several leather pockets, the buttoned flaps of which he felt carefully, regardless of the stream of threats and imprecations that poured from our victim's swollen lips. From the front pockets he proceeded to the back, passing an exploratory hand under the writhing body.

"Ah!" he exclaimed suddenly, "just turn him over, and look out for his heels."

We rolled our captive over, and as Thorndyke "skinned the rabbit," a central pocket came into view, into which, when he had unbuttoned it, he inserted his fingers. "Yes," he continued, "I think this is what we are looking for." He withdrew his fingers, between which he held a small packet of Japanese paper, and with feverish excitement I watched him open out layer after layer of the soft wrapping. As he turned back the last fold a wonderful crimson sparkle told me that the "great ruby" was found.

"There, Jervis," said Thorndyke, holding the magnificent gem towards me in the palm of his hand, "look on this beautiful, sinister thing, charged with untold potentialities of evil – and thank the gods that it is not yours."

He wrapped it up again carefully and, having bestowed it in an inner pocket, said, "And now give me the pistol and run down to the telegraph office and see if you can stop Miller. I should like him to have the credit for this."

I handed him the pistol and made my way out into Fetter Lane and so down to Fleet Street, where at the post office my urgent message was sent off to Scotland Yard immediately. In a few minutes the reply came that Superintendent Miller had not yet left and that he was starting immediately for Clifford's Inn. A quarter of an hour later he drove up in a hansom to the Fetters Lane gate and I conducted him up to the second floor, where Thorndyke introduced him to his prisoner and witnessed the official arrest.

"You don't see how I arrived at it," said Thorndyke as we walked homeward after returning the key. "Well, I am not surprised. The initial evidence was of the weakest; it acquired significance only by cumulative effect. Let us reconstruct it as it developed.

"The derelict hat was, of course, the starting-point. Now, the first thing one noticed was that it appeared to have had more than one owner. No man would buy a new hat that fitted so badly as to need all that packing; and the arrangement of the packing suggested a long-headed man wearing a hat that had belonged to a man with a short head. Then there were the suggestions offered by the slips of paper. The fragmentary address referred to a place the name of which ended in ' n' and the remainder was evidently 'London, W.C.' Now what West Central place names end in 'n'? It was not a street, a square or a court, and Barbican is not in the W.C. district. It was almost certainly one of the half- dozen surviving Inns of Court or Chancery. But, of course, it was not necessarily the address of the owner of the hat.

"The other slip of paper bore the end of a word ending in 'el,' and another word ending in 'eep,' and connected with these were quantities stated in ounces and pennyweights troy weight. But the only persons who I troy weight are those who deal in precious metals. I inferred therefore that the 'el' was part of 'lemel,' and that the 'eep ' was part of 'floor-sweep,' an inference that was supported by the respective quantities, three ounces five pennyweights of lemel and nine and a half ounces of floor-sweep."

"What is lemel?" I asked.

47

"It is the trade name for the gold or silver filings that collect in the 'skin' of a jeweller's bench. Floor-sweep is, of course, the dust swept up on the floor of a jeweller's or goldsmith's workshop. The lemel is actual metal, though not of uniform fineness, but the sweep is a mixture of dirt and metal. Both are saved and sent to the refiners to have the gold and silver extracted.

"This paper, then, was connected either with a gold smith or a gold refiner – who might call himself an assayist or a metallurgist. The connection was supported by the leaf of a price list of gas stoves. A metallurgist would be kept well supplied with lists of gas stoves and furnaces. The traces of lead in the dust from the hat gave us another straw blowing the same direction, for gold assayed by the dry process is fused in the cupel furnace with lead; and as the lead oxidises and the oxide is volatile, traces of lead would tend to appear in the dust deposited in the laboratory.

"The next thing to do was to consult the directory; and when I did so, I found that there were no goldsmiths in any of the Inns and only one assayist – Mr. Highley, of Clifford's Inn. The probabilities therefore, slender as they were, pointed to some connection between this stray hat and Mr. Highley. And this was positively all the information that we had when we came out this afternoon.

"As soon as we got to Clifford's Inn, however, the evidence began to grow like a rolling snowball. First there was Larkin's contribution; and then there was the discovery of the missing hat. Now, as soon as I saw that hat my suspicions fell upon the man upstairs. I felt a conviction that the hat had been left there purposely and that the letter to Larkin was just a red herring to create a false trail. Nevertheless, the presence of that hat completely confirmed the other evidence. It showed that the apparent connection was a real connection."

"But," I asked, "what made you suspect the man upstairs?"

"My dear Jervis!" he exclaimed, "consider the facts. That hat was enough to hang the man who left it there. Can you imagine this astute, wary villain making such an idiot's mistake – going away and leaving the means of his conviction for anyone to find? But you are forgetting that whereas the missing hat was found on the first floor, the murderer's hat was connected with the second floor. The evidence suggested that it was Highley's hat. And now, before we go on to the next stage, let me remind you of those finger-prints. Miller thought that their rough appearance was due to the surface on which they had been made, But it was not. They were the prints of a person who was suffering from ichthyosis, palmar psoriasis or sonic dry dermatitis.

"There is one other point. The man we were looking for was a murderer. His life was already forfeit. To such a man another murder more or less is of no consequence. If this man, having laid the false trail, had determined to take sanctuary in Highley's rooms, it was probable that he had already got rid of Highley. And remember that a metallurgist has unrivalled means disposing of a body; for not only is each of his muffle furnaces a miniature crematorium, but the very residue of a cremated body – bone-ash – is one of the materials of his trade.

"When we went upstairs, I first took the reading of the gas meter and ascertained that a large amount of gas had been used recently. Then, when we entered I took the opportunity to shake hands with Mr. Sherwood, and immediately I became aware that he suffered from a rather extreme form of ichthyosis. That was the first point of verification. Then we discovered that he actually could not distinguish between iron pyrites and auriferous quartz. He was not a metallurgist at all. He was a masquerader. Then the bone-ash in the tub was mixed with fragments of calcined bone, and the cupels all showed similar fragments. In one of them I could see part of the crown of a tooth. That was pure luck. But observe that by that time I had enough evidence to justify an arrest. The tooth served only to bring the affair to a crisis; and his response to my unspoken accusation saved us the trouble of further search for confirmatory evidence."

"What is not quite clear to me," said I, "is when and why he made away with Highley. As the body has been completely reduced to bone-ash, Highley must have been dead at least some days."

"Undoubtedly," Thorndyke agreed. "I take it that the course of events was like this: The police have been searching eagerly for this man, and every new crime must have made his position more unsafe – for a criminal can never be sure that he has not dropped some clue. It began to be necessary for him to make some arrangements for leaving the country and mean while to have a retreat in case his whereabouts should chance to be discovered. Highley's chambers were admirable for both purposes. Here was a solitary man who seldom had a visitor, and who would probably not be missed for some considerable time; and in those chambers were the means of rapidly and completely disposing of the body. The mere murder would be a negligible detail to this ruffian.

"I imagine that Highley was done to death at least a week ago, and that the murderer did not take up his new tenancy until the body was reduced to ash. With that large furnace in addition to the small ones, this would not take long. When the new premises were ready, he could make a sham disappearance to cover his actual flight later; and you must see how perfectly misleading that sham disappearance was. If the police had discovered that hat in the empty room only a week later, they would have been certain that he had escaped to one of the Baltic ports; and while they were following his supposed tracks, he could have gone off comfortably via Folkestone or Southampton."

"Then you think he had only just moved into Highley's rooms?"

"I should say he moved in last night. The murder of Byramji was probably planned on some information that the murderer had picked up, and as soon as it was accomplished he began forthwith to lay down the false tracks. When he reached his rooms yesterday afternoon, he must have written the letter to Larkin and gone off at once to the East End to post it. Then he probably had his bushy hair cut short and shaved off his beard and moustache – which would render him quite unrecognisable by Larkin – and moved into Highley's chambers, from which he would have quietly sallied forth in a few days' time to take his passage to the Continent. It was quite a good plan, and but for the accident of taking the wrong hat, would almost certainly have succeeded."

Once every year, on the second of August, there is delivered with unfailing regularity at No. 5A King's Bench Walk a large box of carved sandal-wood filled with the choicest Trichinopoly cheroots and accompanied by an affectionate letter from our late client, Mr. Byramji. For the second of August is the anniversary of the death (in the execution shed at Newgate) of Cornelius Barnett, otherwise known as the "New Jersey Sphinx."

The Magic Casket

It was in the near neighbourhood of King's Road, Chelsea, that chance, aided by Thorndyke's sharp and observant eyes, introduced us to the dramatic story of the Magic Casket. Not that there was anything strikingly dramatic in the opening phase of the affair, nor even in the story of the casket itself. It was Thorndyke who added the dramatic touch, and most of the magic, too; and I record the affair principally as an illustration of his extraordinary capacity for producing odd items of out-of-the-way knowledge and instantly applying them in the most unexpected manner.

Eight o'clock had struck on a misty November night when we turned out of the main road, and, leaving behind the glare of the shop windows, plunged into the maze of dark and narrow streets to the north. The abrupt change impressed us both, and Thorndyke proceeded to moralise on it in his pleasant, reflective fashion.

"London is an inexhaustible place," he mused. "Its variety is infinite. A minute ago we walked in a glare of light, jostled by a multitude. And now look at this little street. It is as dim as a tunnel, and we have got it absolutely to ourselves. Anything might happen in a place like this."

Suddenly he stopped. We were, at the moment, passing a small church or chapel, the west door of which was enclosed in an open porch; and as my observant friend stepped into the latter and stooped, I perceived in the deep shadow against the wall, the object which had evidently caught his eye.

"What is it?" I asked, following him in.

"It is a handbag," he replied; "and the question is, what is it doing here?"

He tried the church door, which was obviously locked, and coming out, looked at the windows.

"There are no lights in the church." said he; "the place is locked up, and there is nobody in sight. Apparently the bag is derelict. Shall we have a look at it?"

Without waiting for an answer, he picked it up and brought it out into the mitigated darkness of the street, where we proceeded to inspect it. But at the first glance it told its own tale; for it had evidently been locked, and it bore unmistakable traces of having been forced open.

"It isn't empty," said Thorndyke. "I think we had better see what is in it. Just catch hold while I get a light."

He handed me the bag while he felt in his pocket for the tiny electric lamp which he made a habit of carrying, and an excellent habit it is. I held the mouth of the bag open while he illuminated the interior, which we then saw to be occupied by several objects neatly wrapped in brown paper. One of these Thorndyke lifted out, and untying the string and removing the paper, displayed a Chinese stoneware jar. Attached to it was a label, bearing the stamp of the Victoria and Albert Museum, on which was written:

"Miss MABEL BONNET,

168 Willow Walk, Fulham Road, W."

"That tells us all that we want to know," said Thorndyke, re-wrapping the jar and tenderly replacing it in the bag. "We can't do wrong in delivering the things to their owner, especially as the bag itself is evidently her property, too," and he pointed to the gilt initials, "M. B.," stamped on the morocco.

It took us but a few minutes to reach the Fulham Road, but we then had to walk nearly a mile along that thoroughfare before we arrived at Willow Walk – to which an obliging shopkeeper had directed us – and, naturally, No. 168 was at the farther end.

As we turned into the quiet street we almost collided with two men, who were walking at a rapid pace, but both looking back over their shoulders. I noticed that they were both Japanese – well-dressed, gentlemanly- looking men – but I gave them little attention, being interested, rather, in what they were looking at. This was a taxicab which was dimly visible by the light of a street lamp at the farther end of the "Walk," and from which four persons had just alighted. Two of these had hurried ahead to knock at a door, while the other two walked very slowly across the pavement and up the steps to the threshold. Almost immediately the door was opened; two of the shadowy figures entered, and the other two returned slowly to the cab and as we came nearer, I could see that these latter were policemen in uniform. I had just time to note this fact when they both got into the cab and were forthwith spirited away.

"Looks like a street accident of some kind," I remarked; and then, as I glanced at the number of the house we were passing, I added: "Now, I wonder if that house happens to be – yes, by Jove! it is. It is 168! Things have been happening, and this bag of ours is one of the dramatis personae."

The response to our knock was by no means prompt. I was, in fact, in the act of raising my hand to the knocker to repeat the summons when the door opened and revealed an elderly servant-maid, who regarded us inquiringly, and, as I thought, with something approaching alarm.

"Does Miss Mabel Bonney live here?" Thorndyke asked.

"Yes, sir," was the reply; "but I am afraid you can't see her just now, unless it is something urgent. She is rather upset, and particularly engaged at present."

"There is no occasion whatever to disturb her," said Thorndyke. "We have merely called to restore this bag, which seemed to have been lost;" and with this he held it out towards her. She grasped it eagerly with a cry of surprise, and as the mouth fell open, she peered into it.

"Why," she exclaimed, "they don't seem to have taken anything, after all, Where did you find it, sir?"

In the porch of a church in Spelton Street," Thorndyke replied, and was turning away when the servant said earnestly: "Would you kindly give me your name and address, sir? Miss Bonney will wish to write and thank you."

"There is really no need," said he; but she interrupted anxiously: "If you would be so kind, sir. Miss Bonney will be so vexed if she is unable to thank you; and besides, she may want to ask you some questions about it."

"That is true," said Thorndyke (who was restrained only by good manners from asking one or two questions, himself). He produced his card-case, and having handed one of his cards to the maid, wished her " good- evening" and retired.

"That bag had evidently been pinched," I remarked, as we walked back towards the Fulham Road.

"Evidently," he agreed, and was about to enlarge on the matter when our attention was attracted to a taxi, which was approaching from the direction of the main road. A man's head was thrust out of the window, and as the vehicle passed a street lamp, I observed that the head appertained to an elderly gentleman with very white hair and a very fresh face.

"Did you see who that was?" Thorndyke asked.

"It looked like old Brodribb," I replied.

"It did; very much. I wonder where he is of to."

He turned and followed, with a speculative eye, the receding taxi, which presently swept alongside the kerb and stopped, apparently opposite the house from we had just come. As the vehicle came to rest, the door flew open and the passenger shot out like an elderly, but agile, Jack-in-the-box, and bounced up the steps.

"That is Brodribb's knock, sure enough," said I, as the old-fashioned flourish reverberated up the quiet street. "I have heard it too often on our own knocker to mistake it. But we had better not let him see us watching him."

As we went once more on our way, I took a sly glance, now and again, at my friend, noting with a certain malicious enjoyment his profoundly cogitative air. I knew quite well what was happening in his mind for his mind reacted to observed facts in an invariable manner. And here was a group of related facts: the bag, stolen, but deposited intact; the museum label; the injured or sick person – probably Miss Bonney, her self – brought home under police escort; and the arrival, post-haste, of the old lawyer; a significant group of facts. And there was Thorndyke, under my amused and attentive observation, fitting them together in various combinations to see what general conclusion emerged. Apparently my own mental state was equally clear to him, for he remarked, presently, as if response to an unspoken comment: "Well, I expect we shall know all about it before many days have passed if Brodribb sees my card, as he most probably will. Here comes an omnibus that will suit us. Shall we hop on?"

He stood at the kerb and raised his stick; and as the accommodation on the omnibus was such that our seats were separated, there was no opportunity to pursue the subject further, even if there had been anything to discuss.

But Thorndyke's prediction was justified sooner than I had expected. For we had not long finished our supper, and had not yet closed the "oak," when there was heard a mighty flourish on the knocker of our inner door.

"Brodribb, by Jingo!" I exclaimed, and hurried across the room to let him in.

"No, Jervis," he said as I invited him to enter, "I am not coming in. Don't want to disturb you at this time of night. I've just called to make an appointment for to-morrow with a client."

"Is the client's name Bonney?" I asked.

He started and gazed at me in astonishment. "Gad, Jervis!" he exclaimed, "you are getting as bad as Thorndyke. How the deuce did you know that she was my client?"

"Never mind how I know. It is our business to know everything in these chambers. But if your appointment concerns Miss Mabel Bonney, for the Lord's sake come in and give Thorndyke a chance of a night's rest. At present, he is on broken bottles, as Mr. Bumble would express it."

On this persuasion, Mr. Brodribb entered, nothing loath – very much the reverse, in fact – and having bestowed a jovial greeting on Thorndyke, glanced approvingly round the room.

"Ha!" said he, "you look very cosy. If you are really sure I am not–"

I cut him short by propelling him gently towards the fire, beside which I deposited him in an easy chair, while Thorndyke pressed the electric bell which rang up in the laboratory.

"Well," said Brodribb, spreading himself out comfortably before the fire like a handsome old Tom-cat, "if you are going to let me give you a few particulars – but perhaps you would rather that I should not talk shop?"

"Now you know perfectly well, Brodribb," said Thorndyke, "that 'shop' is the breath of life to us all. Let us have those particulars."

Brodribb sighed contentedly and placed his toes on the fender (and at this moment the door opened softly and Polton looked into the room. He took s single, understanding glance at our visitor, and withdrew, shutting the door without a sound).

I am glad," pursued Brodribb, "to have this opportunity of a preliminary chat, because there are certain things that one can say better when the client is not present; and I am deeply interested in Bonney's affairs. The crisis in those affairs which has brought me here is of quite recent date – in fact, it dates from this evening. But I know your partiality for having events related in their proper sequence, so I will leave today's happenings for the moment and tell you the story – the whole of which is material to the case – from the beginning."

Here there was a slight interruption, due to Polton's noiseless entry with a tray on which was a decanter, a biscuit box, and three port glasses. This he deposited, on a small table, which he placed within convenient reach of our guest. Then, with a glance of altruistic satisfaction at our old friend, he stole out like a benevolent ghost.

Dear, dear!" exclaimed Brodribb, beaming on the decanter, "this is really too bad. You ought not to indulge me in this way."

"My dear Brodribb," replied Thorndyke, "you are a benefactor to us. You give us a pretext for taking a glass of port. We can't drink alone, you know."

"I should, if I had a cellar like yours," chuckled Brodribb, sniffing ecstatically at his glass. He took a sip, with his eyes closed, savoured it solemnly, shook his head, and set the glass down on the table.

"To return to our case," he resumed; "Miss Bonney is the daughter of a solicitor, Harold Bonney – you may remember him. He had offices in Bedford Row; and there, one morning, a client came to him and asked him to take care of some property while he, the said client, ran over to Paris, where he had some urgent business. The property in question was a collection of pearls of most unusual size and value, forming a great necklace, which had been unstrung for the sake of portability. It is not clear where they came from, but as the transaction occurred soon after the Russian Revolution, we may make a guess. At any rate, there they were, packed loosely in a leather bag, the string of which was sealed with the owner's seal.

"Bonney seems to have been rather casual about the affair. He gave the client a receipt for the bag, stating the nature of the contents, which he had not seen, and deposited it, in the client's presence, in the safe in his private office. Perhaps he intended to take it to the bank or transfer it to his strong-room, but it is evident that he did neither; for his managing clerk, who kept the second key of the strong-room – without which the room could not be opened – knew nothing of the transaction. When he went home at about seven o'clock, he left Bonney hard at work in his office, and there is no doubt that the pearls were still in the safe.

That night, at about a quarter to nine, it happened that a couple of C.I.D. officers were walking up Bedford Row when they saw three men come out of one of the houses. Two of them turned up towards Theobald's Road, but the third came south, towards them. As he passed them, they both recognised him as a Japanese named Uyenishi, who was believed to be a member of a cosmopolitan gang and whom the police were keeping under observation. Naturally, their suspicions were aroused. The first two men had hurried round the corner and were out of sight; and when they turned to look after Uyenishi, he had mended his pace considerably and was looking back at them. Thereupon one of the officers, named Barker, decided to follow the Jap, while the other, Holt, reconnoitred the premises.

"Now, as soon as Barker turned, the Japanese broke into a run. It was just such a night as this dark and, slightly foggy. In order to keep his man in sight, he had to run, too; and he found that he had a sprinter to deal with. From the bottom of Bedford Row, Uyenishi darted across and shot down Hand Court like a lamp- lighter. Barker followed, but at the Holborn end his man was nowhere to be seen. However, he presently learned from a man at a shop door that the fugitive had run past and turned up Brownlow Street, so off he went again in pursuit. But when he got to the top of the street, back in Bedford Row, he was done. There was no sign of the man, and no one about from whom he could make inquiries. All he could do was to cross the road and walk up Bedford Row to see if Holt had made any discoveries.

"As he was trying to identify the house, his colleague came out on to the doorstep and beckoned him in and this was the story that he told. He had recognised the house by the big lamp-standard; and as the place was all dark, he had gone into the entry and tried the office door. Finding it unlocked, he had entered the clerks' office, lit the gas, and tried the door of the private office, but found it locked. He knocked at it, but getting no answer, had a good look round the clerk's office; and there, presently, on the floor in a dark corner, he found a key. This he tried in the door of the private office, and finding that it fitted, turned it and opened the door. As he did so, the light from the outer office fell on the body of a man lying on the floor just inside.

"A moment's inspection showed that the man had been murdered – first knocked on the head and then finished with a knife. Examination of the pockets showed that the dead man was Harold Bonney, and also that no robbery from the person seemed to have been committed. Nor was there any sign of any other kind of robbery. Nothing seemed to have been disturbed, and the safe had not been broken into, though that was not very conclusive, as the safe key was in the dead man's pocket. However, a murder had been committed, and obviously Uyenishi was either the murderer or an accessory; so Holt had, at once, rung up Scotland Yard on the office telephone, giving all the particulars.

"I may say at once that Uyenishi disappeared completely and at once. He never went to his lodgings at Limehouse, for the police were there before he could have arrived. A lively hue and cry was kept up. Photographs of the wanted man were posted outside every police-station, and a watch was set at all the ports. But he was never found. He must have got away at once on some outward-bound tramp from the Thames. And there we will leave him for the moment.

"At first it was thought that nothing had been stolen, since the managing clerk could not discover that any thing was missing. But a few days later the client returned from Paris, and presenting his receipt, asked for his pearls. But the pearls had vanished. Clearly they had been the object of the crime. The robbers must have known about them and traced them to the office. Of course the safe had been opened with its own key, which was then replaced in the dead man's pocket.

"Now, I was poor Bonney's executor, and in that capacity I denied his liability in respect of the pearls on the ground that he was a gratuitous bailee – there being no evidence that any consideration had been demanded – and that being murdered cannot be construed as negligence. But Miss Mabel, who was practically the sole legatee, insisted on accepting liability. She said that the pearls could have been secured in the bank or the strong-room, and that she was morally, if not legally, liable for their loss; and she insisted on handing to the owner the full amount at which he valued them. It was a wildly foolish proceeding, for he would certainly have accepted half the sum. But still I take my hat off to a person – man or woman – who can accept poverty in preference to a broken covenant"; and here Brodribb, being in fact that sort of person himself, had to be consoled with a replenished glass.

"And mind you," he resumed, "when I speak of poverty, I wish to be taken literally. The estimated value of those pearls was fifty thousand pounds – if you can imagine anyone out of Bedlam giving such a sum for a parcel of trash like that; and when poor Mabel Bonney had paid it, she was left with the prospect of having to spread her butter mighty thin for the rest of her life. As a matter of fact, she has had to sell one after another of her little treasures to pay just her current expenses, and I'm hanged if I can see how she is going to carry on when she has sold the last of them. But there, I mustn't take up your time with her private troubles. Let us return to our muttons.

"First, as to the pearls They were never traced, and it seems probable that they were never disposed of. For, you see, pearls are different from any other kind of gems. You can cut up a big diamond, but you can't cut up a big pearl. And the great value of this necklace was due not only to the size, the perfect shape and 'orient' of the separate pearls, but to the fact that the whole set was perfectly matched. To break up the necklace was to destroy a good part of its value.

"And now as to our friend Uyenishi. He disappeared, as I have said; but he reappeared at Los Angeles, in custody of the police, charged with robbery and murder. He was taken red-handed and was duly convicted and sentenced to death; but for some reason – or more probably, for no reason, as we should think – the sentence was commuted to imprisonment for life. Under these circumstances, the English police naturally took no action, especially as they really had no evidence against him.

"Now Uyenishi was, by trade, a metal-worker; a maker of those pretty trifles that are so dear to the artistic Japanese, and when he was in prison he was allowed to set up a little workshop and practise his trade on a small scale. Among other things that he made was a little casket in the form of a seated figure, which he said he wanted to give to his brother as a keepsake. I don't know whether any permission was granted for him to make this gift, but that is of no consequence; for Uyenishi got influenza and was carried off in a few days by pneumonia; and the prison authorities learned that his brother had been killed, a week or two previously, in a shooting affair at San Francisco. So the casket remained on their hands.

"About this time, Miss Bonney was invited to accompany an American lady on a visit to California, and accepted gratefully. While she was there she paid a visit to the prison to inquire whether Uyenishi had ever made any kind of statement concerning the missing pearls. Here she heard of Uyenishi's recent death; and the governor of the prison, as he could not give her any information, handed over to her the casket as a sort of memento. This transaction came to the knowledge of the press, and – well, you know what the Californian press is like. There were 'some comments,' as they would say, and quite an assortment of Japanese, of shady antecedents, applied to the prison to have the casket 'restored' to them as Uyenishi's heirs. Then Miss Bonney's rooms at the hotel were raided by burglars – but the casket was in the hotel strong-room – and Miss Bonney and her hostess were shadowed by various undesirables in such a disturbing fashion that the two ladies became alarmed and secretly made their way to New York. But there another burglary occurred, with the same unsuccessful result, and the shadowing began again. Finally, Miss Bonney, feeling that her presence was a danger to her friend, decided to return to England, and managed to get on board the ship without letting her departure be known in advance.

"But even in England she has not been left in peace. She has had an uncomfortable feeling of being watched and attended, and has seemed to be constantly meeting Japanese men in the streets, especially in the vicinity of her house. Of course, all the fuss is about this infernal casket; and when she told me what was happening, I promptly popped the thing in my pocket and took it, to my office, where I stowed it in the strong-room. And there, of course, it ought to have remained. but it didn't. One day Miss Bonney told me that she was sending some small things to a loan exhibition of oriental works of art at the South Kensington Museum, and she wished to include the casket. I urged her strongly to do nothing of the kind, but she persisted; and the end of it was that we went to the museum together, with her pottery and stuff in a handbag and the casket in my pocket.

"It was a most imprudent thing to do, for there the beastly casket was, for several months, exposed in a glass case

63

for anyone to see, with her name on the label; and what was worse, full particulars of the origin of the thing. However, nothing happened while it was there – the museum is not an easy place to steal from – and all went well until it was time to remove the things after the close of the exhibition. Now, to-day was the appointed day, and, as on the previous occasion, she and I went to the museum together. But the unfortunate thing is that we didn't come away together. Her other exhibits were all pottery, and these were dealt with first, so that she had her handbag packed and was ready to go before they had begun on the metal work cases. As we were not going the same way, it didn't seem necessary for her to wait; so she went off with her bag and I stayed behind until the casket was released, when I put it in my pocket and went borne, where I locked the thing up again in the strong-room.

"It was about seven when I got borne. A little after eight I heard the telephone ring down in the office, and down I went, cursing the untimely ringer, who turned out to be a policeman at St. George's Hospital. He said he bad found Miss Bonney lying unconscious in the street and had taken her to the hospital, where she had been detained for a while, but she was now recovered and he was taking her home. She would like me, if possible, to go and see her at once. Well, of course, I set off forthwith and got to her house a few minutes after her arrival, and just after you bad left.

"She was a good deal upset, so I didn't worry her with many questions, but she gave me a short account of her misadventure, which amounted to this: She had started to walk home from the museum along the Brompton Road, and she was passing down a quiet street between that and Fulham Road when she heard soft footsteps behind her. The next moment, a scarf or shawl was thrown over her head and drawn tightly round her neck. At the same moment, the bag was snatched from her hand. That is all that she remembers, for she was half and so terrified that she fainted, and knew no more until she found herself in a cab with two policemen who were taking her to the hospital.

"Now it is obvious that her assailants were in search of that damned casket, for the bag had been broken open and searched, but nothing taken or damaged; which suggests the Japanese again, for a British thief would have smashed the crockery. I found your card there, and I put it to Miss Bonney that we had better ask you to help us – I told her all about you – and she agreed emphatically. So that is why I am here, drinking your port and robbing you of your night's rest."

"And what do you want me to do?" Thorndyke asked.

"Whatever you think best," was the cheerful reply. "In the first place, this nuisance must be put a stop to – this shadowing and hanging about. But apart from that, you must see that there is something queer about this accursed casket. The beastly thing is of no intrinsic value. The museum man turned up his nose at it. But it evidently has some extrinsic value, and no small value either. If it is good enough for these devils to follow it all the way from the States, as they seem to have done, it is good enough for us to try to find out what its value is. That is where you come in. I propose to bring Miss Bonney to see you to-morrow, and I will bring the infernal casket, too. Then you will ask her a few questions, take a look at the casket – through the microscope, if necessary – and tell us all about it in your usual necromantic way."

Thorndyke laughed as he refilled our friend's glass. "If faith will move mountains, Brodribb," said he, "you ought to have been a civil engineer. But it is certainly a rather intriguing problem."

"Ha!" exclaimed the old solicitor; "then it's all right. I've known you a good many years, but I've never known you to be stumped; and you are not going to be stumped now. What time shall I bring her? Afternoon or evening would suit her best."

"Very well," replied Thorndyke; "bring her to tea – say, five o'clock. How will that do?"

"Excellently; and here's good luck to the adventure." He drained his glass, and the decanter being now empty, he rose, shook our hands warmly, and took his departure in high spirits.

It was with a very lively interest that I looked for ward to the prospective visit. Like Thorndyke, I found the case rather intriguing. For it was quite clear, as our shrewd old friend had said, that there was something more than met the eye in the matter of this casket.

Hence, on the following afternoon, when, on the stroke of five, footsteps became audible on our stairs, I awaited the arrival of our new client with keen curiosity, both as to herself and her mysterious property.

To tell the truth, the lady was better worth looking at than the casket. At the first glance, I was strongly prepossessed in her favour, and so, I think, was Thorndyke. Not that she was a beauty, though comely enough. But she was an example of a type that seems to be growing rarer; quiet, gentle, soft-spoken, and a lady to her finger-tips; a little sad-faced and care worn, with a streak or two of white in her prettily- disposed black hair, though she could not have been much over thirty-five. Altogether a very gracious and winning personality.

When we had been presented to her by Brodribb – who treated her as if she had been a royal personage- and had enthroned her in the most comfortable easy- chair, we inquired as to her health, and were duly thanked for the salvage of the bag. Then Polton brought in the tray, with an air that seemed to demand an escort of choristers; the tea was poured out, and the informal proceedings began.

She had not, however, much to tell; for she had not seen her assailants, and the essential facts of the case had been fully presented in Brodribb's excellent summary. After a very few questions, therefore, we came to the next stage; which was introduced by Brodribb's taking from his pocket a small parcel which he proceeded to open.

There," said he, "that is the *fons et origo mali*. Not much to look at, I think you will agree." He set the object down on the table and glared at it malevolently, while Thorndyke and I regarded it with a more impersonal interest. It was not much to look at. Just an ordinary Japanese casket in the form of a squat, shapeless figure with a silly little grinning face, of which the head and shoulders opened on a hinge; a pleasant enough object, with its quiet, warm colouring, but certainly not a masterpiece of art.

Thorndyke picked it up and turned it over slowly for preliminary inspection; then he went on to examine it detail by detail, watched closely, in his turn, by Brodribb and me. Slowly and methodically, his eye – fortified by a watchmaker's eyeglass – travelled over every part of the exterior. Then he opened it, and I having examined the inside of the lid, scrutinised the bottom from within, long and attentively. Finally, he turned the casket upside down and examined the bottom from without, giving to it the longest and most rigorous inspection of all – which puzzled me somewhat, for the bottom was absolutely plain At length, he passed the casket and the eyeglass to me without comment.

"Well," said Brodribb, "what is the verdict?"

"It is of no value as a work of art," replied Thorndyke. "The body and lid are just castings of common white metal – an antimony alloy, I should say. The bronze colour is lacquer."

"So the museum man remarked." said Brodribb.

"But," continued Thorndyke, "there is one very odd thing about it. The only piece of fine metal in it is in the part which matters least. The bottom is a separate plate of the alloy known to the Japanese as Shakudo – an alloy of copper and gold."

"Yes," said Brodribb, "the museum man noted that, too, and couldn't make out why it had been put there."

"Then," Thorndyke continued, "there is another anomalous feature; the inside of the bottom is covered with elaborate decoration – just the place where decoration is most inappropriate, since it would be covered up by the contents of the casket. And, again, this decoration is etched; not engraved or chased. But etching is a very unusual process for this purpose, if it is ever used at all by Japanese metal-workers. My impression is that it is not; for it is most unsuitable for decorative purposes. That is all that I observe, so far."

"And what do you infer from your observations?" Brodribb asked.

I should like to think the matter over," was the reply. "There is an obvious anomaly, which must have some significance. But I won't embark on speculative opinions at this stage. I should like, however, to take one or two photographs of the casket, for reference; but that will occupy some time. You will hardly want to wait so long."

"No," said Brodribb. "But Miss Bonney is coming with me to my office to go over some documents and discuss a little business. When we have finished, I will come back and fetch the confounded thing."

"There is no need for that," replied Thorndyke. "As soon as I have done what is necessary, I will bring it up to your place."

To this arrangement Brodribb agreed readily, and he and his client prepared to depart. I rose, too, and as I happened to have a call to make in Old Square, Lincoln's Inn, I asked permission to walk with them.

As we came out into King's Bench Walk I noticed a smallish, gentlemanly-looking man who had just passed our entry and now turned in at the one next door; and by the light of the lamp in the entry he looked to me like a Japanese. I thought Miss Bonney had observed him, too, but she made no remark, and neither did I. But, passing up Inner Temple Lane, we nearly overtook two other men, who – though I got but a back view of them and the light was feeble enough – aroused my suspicions by their neat, small figures. As we approached, they quickened their pace, and one of them looked back over his shoulder; and then my suspicions were confirmed, for it was an unmistakable Japanese face that looked round at us. Miss Bonney saw that I had observed the men, for she remarked, as they turned sharply at the Cloisters and entered Pump Court: "You see, I am still haunted by Japanese."

"I noticed them," said Brodribb. "They are probably law students. But we may as well be companionable"; and with this, he, too, headed for Pump Court.

We followed our oriental friends across the Lane into Fountain Court, and through that and Devereux Court out to Temple Bar, where we parted from them; they turning westward and we crossing to Bell Yard, up which we walked, entering New Square by the Carey Street gate. At Brodribb's doorway we halted and looked back, but no one was in sight. I accordingly went my way, promising to return anon to hear Thorndyke's report, and the lawyer and his client disappeared through the portal.

My business occupied me longer than I had expected, I but nevertheless, when I arrived at Brodribb's premises – where he lived in chambers over his office – Thorndyke had not yet made his appearance. A quarter of an hour later, however, we heard his brisk step on the stairs, and as Brodribb threw the door open, he entered and produced the casket from his pocket.

"Well," said Brodribb, taking it from him and locking it, for the time being, in a drawer, "has the oracle Spoken; and if so, what did he say?"

"Oracles," replied Thorndyke, "have a way of being more concise than explicit. Before I attempt to interpret the message, I should like to view the scene of the escape; to see if there was any intelligible reason why this man Uyenishi should have returned up Brownlow Street into what must have been the danger zone. I think that is a material question."

69

"Then," said Brodribb, with evident eagerness, "let us all walk up and have a look at the confounded place. It is quite close by."

We all agreed instantly, two of us, at least, being on the tip-toe of expectation. For Thorndyke, who habitually understated his results, had virtually admitted that the casket had told him something; and as we walked up the Square to the gate in Lincoln's Inn Fields, I watched him furtively, trying to gather from his impassive face a hint as to what the something amounted to, and wondering how the movements of the fugitive bore on the solution of the mystery. Brodribb was similarly occupied, and as we crossed from Great Turnstile and took our way up Brownlow Street, I could see that his excitement was approaching bursting-point.

At the top of the street Thorndyke paused and looked up and down the rather dismal thoroughfare which forms a continuation of Bedford Row and bears its name. Then he crossed to the paved island surrounding the pump which stands in the middle of the road, and from thence surveyed the entrances to Brownlow Street and Hand Court; and then he turned and looked thoughtfully at the pump.

"A quaint old survivor, this," he remarked, tapping the iron shell with his knuckles. "There is a similar one, you may remember, in Queen Square, and another at Aldgate. But that is still in use."

"Yes," Brodribb assented, almost dancing with impatience and inwardly damning the pump, as I could see, "I've noticed it."

I suppose," Thorndyke proceeded, in a reflective tone, "they had to remove the handle. But it was rather a pity."

"Perhaps it was," growled Brodribb, whose complexion was rapidly developing affinities to that of a pickled cabbage, " but what the d—"

Here he broke off short and glared silently at Thorndyke, who had raised his arm and squeezed his hand into the opening once occupied by the handle. He groped in the interior with an expression of placid interest, and presently reported: "The barrel is still there, and so, apparently, is the plunger " – (Here I heard Brodribb mutter huskily, "Damn the barrel and the plunger too!") "but my hand is rather large for the exploration. Would you, Miss Bonney, mind slipping your hand in and telling me if I am right?"

We all gazed at Thorndyke in dismay, but in a moment Miss Bonney recovered from her astonishment, and with a deprecating smile, half shy, half amused, she slipped off her glove, and reaching up – it was rather high for her – inserted her hand into the narrow slit. Brodribb glared at her and gobbled like a turkey-cock, and I watched her with a sudden suspicion that something was going to happen. Nor was I mistaken. For, as I looked, the shy, puzzled smile faded from her face and was succeeded by an expression of incredulous astonishment. Slowly she withdrew her hand, and as it came out of the slit it dragged something after it. I started forward, and by the light of the lamp above the pump I could see that the object was a leather bag secured by a string from which hung a broken seal.

"It can't be!" she gasped as, with trembling fingers, she untied the string. Then, as she peered into the open mouth, she uttered a little cry. "It is! It is! It is the necklace!"

Brodribb was speechless with amazement. So was I; and I was still gazing open-mouthed at the bag in Miss Bonney's hands when I felt Thorndyke touch my arm. I turned quickly and found him offering me an automatic pistol. "Stand by, Jervis," he said quietly, looking towards Gray's Inn.

I looked in the same direction, and then perceived three men stealing round the corner from Jockey' Fields. Brodribb saw them, too, and snatching the bag of pearls from his client's hands, buttoned it into his breast pocket and placed himself before its owner, grasping his stick with a war-like air. The three men filed along the pavement until they were opposite us, when they turned simultaneously and bore down on the pump, each man, as I noticed, holding his right hand behind him. In a moment, Thorndyke's hand, grasping a pistol, flew up – as did mine, also – and he called out sharply: "Stop! If any man moves a hand, I fire."

The challenge brought them up short, evidently unprepared for this kind of reception. What would have happened next it is impossible to guess. But at this moment a police whistle sounded and two constables ran out from Hand Court. The whistle was instantly echoed from the direction of Warwick Court, whence two more constabulary figures appeared through the postern gate of Gray's Inn. Our three attendants hesitated but for an instant. Then, with one accord, they turned tail and flew like the wind round into Jockey's Fields, with the whole posse of constables close on their heels.

"Remarkable coincidence," said Brodribb, "that those policemen should happen to be on the look-out. Or isn't it a coincidence?"

"I telephoned to the station superintendent before I started," replied Thorndyke, "warning him of a possible breach of the peace at this spot."

Brodribb chuckled. "You're a wonderful man, Thorndyke. You think of everything. I wonder if the police will catch those fellows."

"It is no concern of ours," replied Thorndyke. "We've got the pearls, and that finishes the business. There will be no more shadowing, in any case."

Miss Bonney heaved a comfortable little sigh and glanced gratefully at Thorndyke. "You can have no idea what a relief that is!" she exclaimed; " to say nothing of the treasure-trove."

We waited some time, but as neither the fugitives nor the constables reappeared, we presently made our way back down

Brownlow Street. And there it was that Brodribb had an inspiration.

"I'll tell you what," said be. "I will just pop these things in my strong-room – they will be perfectly safe there until the bank opens to-morrow – and then we'll go and have a nice little dinner. I'll pay the piper."

"Indeed you won't!" exclaimed Miss Bonney. "This is my thanksgiving festival, and the benevolent wizard shall be the guest of the evening."

"Very well, my dear," agreed Brodribb. "I will pay and charge it to the estate. But I stipulate that the benevolent wizard shall tell us exactly what the oracle said. That is essential to the preservation of my sanity."

"You shall have his *ipissima verba*," Thorndyke promised; and the resolution was carried, *nem. con.*

An hour and a half later we were seated around a table in a private room of a café to which Mr. Brodribb had conducted us. I may not divulge its whereabouts, though I may, perhaps, hint that we approached it by way of Wardour Street. At any rate, we had dined, even to the fulfilment of Brodribb's ideal, and coffee and liqueurs furnished a sort of gastronomic doxology. Brodribb had lighted a cigar and Thorndyke had produced a vicious-looking little black cheroot, which he regarded fondly and then returned to its abiding-place as unsuited to the present company.

"Now," said Brodribb, watching Thorndyke fill his pipe (as understudy of the cheroot aforesaid), "we are waiting to hear the words of the oracle."

"You shall hear them," Thorndyke replied. "There were only five of them. But first, there are certain introductory matters to be disposed of. The solution of this problem is based on two well-known physical facts, one metallurgical and the other optical."

73

"Ha!" said Brodribb. "But you must temper the wind to the shorn lamb, you know, Thorndyke. Miss Bonney and I are not scientists."

"I will put the matter quite simply, but you must have the facts. The first relates to the properties of malleable metals – excepting iron and steel – and especially of copper and its alloys. If a plate of such metal or alloy – say, bronze, for instance – is made red-hot and quenched in water, it becomes quite soft and flexible – the reverse of what happens in the case of iron. Now, if such a plate of softened metal be placed on a steel anvil and hammered, it becomes extremely hard and brittle."

"I follow that," said Brodribb.

"Then see what follows. If, instead of hammering the soft plate, you put on it the edge of a blunt chisel and strike on that chisel a sharp blow, you produce an indented line. Now the plate remains soft; but the metal forming the indented line has been hammered and has become hard. There is now a line of hard metal on the soft plate. Is that clear?"

"Perfectly," replied Brodribb; and Thorndyke accordingly continued: "The second fact is this: If a beam of light falls on a polished surface which reflects it, and if that surface is turned through a given angle, the beam of light is deflected through double that angle."

"H'm!" grunted Brodribb. "Yes. No doubt. I hope we are not going to get into any deeper waters, Thorndyke."

"We are not," replied the latter, smiling urbanely. "We are now going to consider the application of these facts. Have you ever seen a Japanese magic mirror?

"Never; nor even heard of such a thing."

"They are bronze mirrors, just like the ancient Greek or Etruscan mirrors – which are probably 'magic' mirrors, too. A typical specimen consists of a circular or oval plate of bronze, highly polished on the face and decorated on the back with chased ornament – commonly a dragon or some such device – and furnished with a handle. The ornament is, as I have said, chased; that is to say, it is executed in indented lines made with chasing tools, which are, in effect, small chisels, more or less blunt, which are struck with a chasing-hammer.

"Now these mirrors have a very singular property. Although the face is perfectly plain, as a mirror should be, yet, if a beam of sunlight is caught on it and reflected, say, on to a white wall, the round or oval patch of light on the wall is not a plain light patch. It shows quite clearly the ornament on the back of the mirror."

"But how extraordinary!" exclaimed Miss Bonney.

"It sounds quite incredible." I said.

"It does," Thorndyke agreed. "And yet the explanation is quite simple. Professor Sylvanus Thompson pointed it out years ago. It is based on the facts which I have just stated to you. The artist who makes one of these mirrors begins, naturally, by annealing the metal until it is quite soft. Then he chases the design on the back, and this design then shows slightly on the face. But he now grinds the face perfectly flat with fine emery and water so that the traces of the design are complete obliterated. Finally, he polishes the face with rouge on a soft buff.

"But now observe that wherever the chasing-tool has made a line, the metal is hardened right through, so that the design is in hard metal on a soft matrix. But the hardened metal resists the wear of the polishing buffer more than the soft metal does. The result is that the act of polishing causes the design to appear in faint relief on the face. Its projection is infinitesimal – less than the hundred-thousandth of an inch – and totally invisible to the eye. But, minute as it is, owing to the optical law which I mentioned – which, in effect, doubles the projection – it is enough to influence the reflection of light. As a consequence, every chased line appears on the patch of light as a dark line with a bright border, and so the whole design is visible. I think that is quite clear."

"Perfectly clear," Miss Bonney and Brodribb agreed.

"But now," pursued Thorndyke, "before we come to the casket, there is a very curious corollary which I must mention. Supposing our artist, having finished the mirror, should proceed with a scraper to erase the design from the back; and on the blank, scraped surface to etch a new design. The process of etching does not harden the metal, so the new design does not appear on the reflection. But the old design would. For although it was invisible on the face and had been erased from the back, it would still exist in the substance of the metal and continue to influence the reflection. The odd result would be that the design which would be visible in the patch of light on the wall would be a different one from that on the back of the mirror.

"No doubt, you see what I am leading up to. But I will take the investigation of the casket as it actually occurred. It was obvious, at once, that the value of the thing was extrinsic. It had no intrinsic value, either in material or workmanship. What could that value be? The clear suggestion was that the casket was the vehicle of some secret message or information. It had been made by Uyenishi, who had almost certainly had possession of the missing pearls, and who had been so closely pursued that be never had an opportunity to communicate with his confederates. It was to be given to a man who was almost certainly one of those confederates; and, since the pearls had never been traced, there was a distinct probability that the (presumed) message referred to some hiding-place in which Uyenishi had concealed them during his flight, and where they were probably still hidden.

"With these considerations in my mind, I examined the casket, and this was what I found. The thing, itself, was a common white-metal casting, made presentable by means of lacquer. But the white metal bottom had been cut out and replaced by a plate of fine bronze – Shakudo. The inside of this

76

was covered with an etched design, which immediately aroused my suspicions. Turning it over, I saw that the outside of the bottom was not only smooth and polished; it was a true mirror. It gave a perfectly undistorted reflection of my face. At once, I suspected that the mirror held the secret; that the message, whatever it was, had been chased on the back, had then been scraped away and an etched design worked on it to hide the traces of the scraper.

"As soon as you were gone, I took the casket up to the laboratory and threw a strong beam of parallel light from a condenser on the bottom, catching the reflection on a sheet of white paper. The result was just what I had expected. On the bright oval patch on the paper could be seen the shadowy, but quite distinct, forms of five words in the Japanese character.

"I was in somewhat of a dilemma, for I have no knowledge of Japanese, whereas the circumstances were such as to make it rather unsafe to employ a translator. However, as I do just know the Japanese characters and possess a Japanese dictionary, I determined to make an attempt to fudge out the words myself. If I failed, I could then look for a discreet translator.

"However, it proved to be easier than I had expected, for the words were detached; they did not form a sentence, and so involved no questions of grammar. I spelt out the first word and then looked it up in the dictionary. The translation was 'pearls.' This looked hopeful, and I went on to the next, of which the translation was 'pump.' The third word floored me. It seemed to be 'jokkis,' or 'jokkish,' but there was no such word in the dictionary; so I turned to the next word, hoping that it would explain its predecessor. And it did. The fourth word was 'fields,' and the last word was evidently 'London.' So the entire group read 'Pearls, Pump, Jokkis, Fields, London.'

"Now, there is no pump, so far as I know, in Jockey Fields, but there is one in Bedford Row close to the corner of the Fields, and exactly opposite the end of Brownlow Street And by

Mr. Brodribb's account, Uyenishi, in his flight, ran down Hand Court and re turned up Brownlow Street, as if he were making for the pump. As the latter is disused and the handle-hole is high up, well out of the way of children, it offers quite a good temporary hiding-place, and I had no doubt that the bag of pearls had been poked into it and was probably there still. I was tempted to go at once and explore; but I was anxious that the discovery should be made by Miss Bonney, herself, and I did not dare to make a preliminary exploration for fear of being shadowed. If I had found the treasure I should have had to take it and give it to her; which would have been a flat ending to the adventure. So I had to dissemble and be the occasion of much smothered objurgation on the part of my friend Brodribb. And that is the whole story of my interview with the oracle."

Our mantelpiece is becoming a veritable museum of trophies of victory, the gifts of grateful clients. Among them is a squat, shapeless figure of a Japanese gentleman of the old school, with a silly grinning little face – The Magic Casket. But its possession is no longer a menace. Its sting has been drawn; its magic is exploded; its secret is exposed, and its glory departed.

The Pathologist to the Rescue

"I hope," said I, as I looked anxiously out of our window up King's Bench Walk, "that our friend, Foxley, will turn up to time, or I shall lose the chance of hearing his story. I must be in court by half-past eleven. The telegram said that he was a parson, didn't it?"

"Yes," replied Thorndyke. "The Reverend Arthur Foxley."

"Then perhaps this may be he. There is a parson crossing from the Row in this direction, only he has a girl with him. He didn't say anything about a girl, did he?"

"No. He merely asked for the appointment. How ever," he added, as he joined me at the window and watched the couple approaching with their eyes apparently fixed on the number above our portico, "this is evidently our client, and punctual to the minute."

In response to the old-fashioned flourish on our little knocker, he opened the inner door and invited the clergyman and his companion to enter; and while the mutual introductions were in progress, I looked critically at our new clients. Mr. Foxley was a typical and favour able specimen of his class: a handsome, refined, elderly gentleman, prim as to his speech, suave and courteous in bearing, with a certain engaging simplicity of manner which impressed me very favourably. His companion I judged to be a parishioner for she was what ladies are apt to describe as "not quite"; that is to say, her social level appeared to appertain to the lower strata of the middle-class. But she was a fine, strapping girl, very sweet-faced and winsome, quiet and gentle in manner and obviously in deep trouble, for her clear grey eyes – fixed earnestly, almost devouringly, on Thorndyke – were reddened and swimming with unshed tears.

"We have sought your aid, Dr. Thorndyke," the clergyman began, "on the advice of my friend, Mr. Brodribb, who happened to call on me on some business. He assured me that you would be able to solve our difficulties if it were humanly possible, so I have come to lay those difficulties before you. I pray to God that you may be able to help us, for my poor young friend here, Miss Markham, is in a most terrible position, as you will understand when I tell you that her future husband, a most admirable young man named Robert Fletcher, is in the custody of the police, charged with robbery and murder."

Thorndyke nodded gravely, and the clergyman continued: "I had better tell you exactly what has happened. The dead man is one Joseph Riggs, a maternal uncle of Fletcher's, a strange, eccentric man, solitary, miserly, and of a violent, implacable temper. He was quite well-to-do, though penurious and haunted constantly by an absurd fear of poverty. His nephew, Robert, was apparently his only known relative, and, under his will, was his sole heir. Recently, however, Robert has become engaged to my friend, Miss Lilian, and this engagement was violently opposed by his uncle, who had repeatedly urged him to make what he called a profitable marriage. For Miss Lilian is a dowerless maiden – dowerless save for those endowments with which God has been pleased to enrich her, and which her future husband has properly prized above mere material wealth. However, Riggs declared, in his brutal way, that he was not going to leave his property to the husband of a shop-woman, and that Robert might look out for a wife with money or be struck out of his will.

"The climax was reached yesterday when Robert, in response to a peremptory summons, went to see his uncle. Mr. Riggs was in a very intractable mood. He demanded that Robert should break off his engagement unconditionally and at once, and when Robert bluntly insisted on his right to choose his own wife the old man worked himself up into a furious rage, shouting, cursing, using the most offensive language and even uttering threats of personal violence. Finally, he drew his gold watch from his pocket and laid it with its chain on the table then, opening a drawer, he took out a bundle of bearer bonds and threw them down by the watch.

"'There, my friend,' said he, that is your inheritance. That is all you will get from me, living or dead. Take it and go, and don't let me ever set eyes on you again.'

"At first Robert refused to accept the gift, but his uncle became so violent that eventually, for peace's sake, he took the watch and the bonds, intending to return them later, and went away. He left at half-past five, leaving his uncle alone in the house."

"How was that?" Thorndyke asked. "Was there no servant?"

"Mr. Riggs kept no resident servant. The young woman who did his housework came at half-past eight in the morning and left at half-past four. Yesterday she waited until five to get tea ready, but then, as the uproar in the sitting-room was still unabated, she thought it best to go. She was afraid to go in to lay the tea-things.

"This morning, when she arrived at the house, she found the front door unlocked, as it always was during the day. On entering, her attention was at once attracted by two or three little pools of blood on the floor of the hall, or passage. Somewhat alarmed by this, she looked into the sitting-room, and finding no one there, and being impressed by the silence in the house, she went along the passage to a back room – a sort of study or office, which was usually kept locked when Mr. Riggs was not in. Now, however, it was unlocked and the door was ajar; so having first knocked and receiving no answer, she pushed open the door and looked in; and there, to her horror, she saw her employer lying on the floor, apparently dead, with a wound on the side of his head and a pistol on the floor by his side.

"Instantly she turned and rushed out of the house, and she was running up the street in search of a police man when she encountered me at a corner and burst out with her dreadful tidings. 1 walked with her to the police station, and as we went she told me what had happened on the previous afternoon. Naturally, I was profoundly shocked and also alarmed, for I saw that – rightly or wrongly – suspicion must immediately fail on Robert Fletcher. The servant, Rose Turnmill, took it for granted that he had murdered her master; and when we found the station inspector, and Rose had repeated her statement to him, it was evident that he took the same view.

"With him and a sergeant, we went back to the house; but on the way we met Mr. Brodribb, who was staying at the 'White Lion' and had just come out for a walk. I told him, rapidly, what had occurred and begged him to come with us, which, with the inspector's consent, he did; and as we walked I explained to him the awful position that Robert Fletcher might be placed in, and asked him to advise me what to do. But, of course, there was nothing to be said or done until we had seen the body and knew whether any suspicion rested on Robert.

"We found the man Riggs lying as Rose had said. He was quite dead, cold and stiff. There was a pistol wound on the right temple, and a pistol lay on the floor at his right side. A little blood – but not much – had trickled from the wound and lay in a small pool on the oilcloth. The door of an iron safe was open and a bunch of keys hung from the lock; and on a desk one or two share certificates were spread out. On searching the dead man's pockets it was found that the gold watch which the servant told us he usually carried was missing, and when Rose went to the bedroom to see if it was there, it was nowhere to be found.

"Apart from the watch, however, the appearances suggested that the man had taken his own life. But against this view was the blood on the hall floor. The dead man appeared to have fallen at once from the effects of the shot, and there had been very little bleeding. Then how came the blood in the hall? The inspector decided that it could not have been the blood of the deceased; and when we examined it and saw that there were several little pools and that they seemed to form a track towards the street door, he was convinced that the blood had fallen from some person who had been wounded and was escaping from the house. And, under the circumstances, he was bound to assume that that person was Robert Fletcher; and on that assumption, he dispatched the sergeant forthwith to arrest Robert.

"On this I held a consultation with Mr. Brodribb, who pointed out that the case turned principally on the blood in the hall. If it was the blood of deceased, and the absence of the watch could be explained, a verdict of suicide could be accepted. But if it was the blood of some other person, that fact would point to murder. The question, he said, would have to be settled, if possible, and his advice to me, if I believed Robert to be innocent – which, from my knowledge of him, I certainly did – was this: Get a couple of small, clean, labelled bottles from a chemist and – with the inspector's consent – put in one a little of the blood from the hall and in the other some of the blood of the deceased. Seal them both in the inspector's presence and mine and take them up to Dr. Thorndyke. If it is possible to answer the question, Are they or are they not from the same person? he will answer it.

"Well, the inspector made no objection, so I did what he advised. And here are the specimens. I trust they may tell us what we want to know."

Here Mr. Foxley took from his attaché-case a small cardboard box, and opening it, displayed two little wide-mouthed bottles carefully packed in cotton wool. Lifting them out tenderly, he placed them on the table before Thorndyke. They were both neatly corked, sealed – with Brodribb's seal, as I noticed – and labelled; the one inscribed "Blood of Joseph

Riggs," and the other "Blood of unknown origin," and both signed "Arthur Foxley" and dated. At the bottom of each was a small mass of gelatinous blood-clot.

Thorndyke looked a little dubiously at the two bottles, and addressing the clergyman, said: "I am afraid Mr. Brodribb has rather over-estimated our resources. There is no known method by which the blood of one person can be distinguished with certainty from that of another."

"Dear, dear!" exclaimed Mr. Foxley. "How disappointing! Then these specimens are useless, after all?"

"I won't say that; but it is in the highest degree improbable that they will yield any information. You must build no expectations on them."

"But you will examine them and see if anything is to be gleaned," the parson urged, persuasively.

"Yes, I will examine them. But you realise that if they should yield any evidence, that evidence might be unfavourable?"

"Yes; Mr. Brodribb pointed that out, but we are willing to take the risk, and so, I may say, is Robert Fletcher, to whom I put the question."

"Then you have seen Mr. Fletcher since the discovery?"

"Yes, I saw him at the police station after his arrest. It was then that he gave me – and also the police – the particulars that I have repeated to you. He had to make a statement, as the dead man's watch and the bonds were found in his possession."

"With regard to the pistol. Has it been identified?"

"No. It is an old-fashioned derringer which no one has ever seen before, so there is no evidence as to whose property it was."

"And as to those share certificates which you spoke of as lying on the desk. Do you happen to remember what they were?"

84

"Yes, they were West African mining shares; Abu sum Pa-pa was the name, I think."

"Then," said Thorndyke," Mr. Riggs had been losing money. The Abusum Pa-pa Company has just gone into liquidation. Do you know if anything had been taken from the safe?"

it is impossible to say, but apparently not, as there was a good deal of money in the cash-box, which we unlocked and inspected. But we shall hear more to-morrow at the inquest, and I trust we shall hear something there from you. But in any case I hope you will attend to watch the proceedings on behalf of poor Fletcher. And if possible, to be present at the autopsy at eleven o'clock. Can you manage that?"

"Yes. And I shall come down early enough to make an inspection of the premises if the police will give the necessary facilities."

Mr. Foxley thanked him effusively, and when the details as to the trains had been arranged, our clients rose to depart. Thorndyke shook their hands cordially, and as he bade farewell to Miss Markham he murmured a few words of encouragement. She looked up at him gratefully and appealingly as she naïvely held his hand.

"You will try to help us, Dr. Thorndyke, won't you?" she urged. "And you will examine that blood very, very carefully. Promise that you will. Remember that poor Robert's life may hang upon what you can tell about it."

I realise that, Miss Markham," he replied gently, "and I promise you that the specimens shall be most thoroughly examined; and further, that no stone shall be left unturned in my endeavours to bring the truth to light."

At his answer, spoken with infinite kindliness and sympathy, her eyes filled and she turned away with a few broken words of thanks, and the good clergyman – himself not unmoved by the little episode – took her arm and led her to the door.

"Well," I remarked as their retreating footsteps died away, "old Brodribb's enthusiasm seems to have let you in for a queer sort of task; and I notice that you appear to have accepted Fletcher's statement."

"Without prejudice," he replied. "I don't know Fletcher, but the balance of probabilities is in his favour. Still, that blood-track in the hall is a curious feature. It certainly requires explanation."

"It does, indeed!" I exclaimed, "and you have got to find the explanation! Well, I wish you joy of the job. I suppose you will carry out the farce to the bitter end as you have promised? "

Certainly," he replied. "But it is hardly a farce. I should have looked the specimens over in any case. One never knows what illuminating fact a chance observation may bring into view."

I smiled sceptically.

"The fact that you are asked to ascertain is that these two samples of blood came from the same person. If there are any means of proving that, they are unknown to me. I should have said it was an impossibility."

"Of course," he rejoined, "you are quite right, speaking academically and in general terms. No method of identifying the blood of individual persons has hitherto been discovered. But yet I can imagine the possibility, in particular and exceptional cases, of an actual, personal identification by means of blood. What does my learned friend think?"

"He thinks that his imagination is not equal to the required effort," I answered; and with that I picked up my brief-bag and went forth to my duties at the courts.

That Thorndyke would keep his promise to poor Lilian Markham was a foregone conclusion, preposterous as the examination seemed. But even my long experience of my colleague's scrupulous conscientiousness had not prepared me for the spectacle which met my eyes when I returned to our chambers. On the table stood the microscope, flanked by three slide-boxes. Each box held six trays, and each tray held six slides – a hundred and eight slides in all!

But why three boxes? I opened one. The slides – carefully mounted blood-films – were labelled "Joseph Riggs." Those in the second box were labelled," Blood from hall floor." But when I opened the third box, I beheld a collection of empty slides labelled "Robert Fletcher"!

I chuckled aloud. Prodigious! Thorndyke was going even one better than his promise. He was not only going to examine – probably had examined – the two samples produced; he was actually going to collect a third sample for himself!

I picked out one of Mr. Riggs's slides and laid it on the stage of the microscope. Thorndyke seemed to have been using a low-power objective – the inch-and-a-half. After a glance through this, I swung round the nose- piece to the high power. And then I got a further surprise. The brightly-coloured "white" corpuscles showed that Thorndyke had actually been to the trouble of staining the films with eosin! Again I murmured, "Prodigious!" and put the slide back in its box. For, of course, it showed just what one expected: blood – or rather, broken-up blood-clot. From its appearance I could not even have sworn that it was human blood.

I had just closed the box when Thorndyke entered the room. His quick eye at once noted the changed objective and he remarked: "I see you have been having a look at the specimens."

"A specimen." I corrected. "Enough is as good as a feast."

"Blessed are they who are easily satisfied," be retorted; and then he added: "I have altered my arrangements, though I needn't interfere with yours. I shall go down to Southaven to-night; in fact, I am starting in a few minutes."

"Why?" I asked.

"For several reasons. I want to make sure of the post-mortem tomorrow morning, I want to pick up any further facts that are available, and finally, I want to prepare a set of blood-films from Robert Fletcher. We may as well make the series complete," he added with a smile, to which I replied by a broad grin.

"Really, Thorndyke," I protested. "I'm surprised at you, at your age, too. She is a nice girl, but she isn't so beautiful as to justify a hundred and eight blood- films."

I accompanied him to the taxi, followed by Polton, who carried his modest luggage, and then returned to speculate on his probable plan of campaign. For, of course, he had one. His purposive, resolute manner told me that he had seen farther into this case than I had. I accepted that as natural and inevitable. Indeed, I may admit that my disrespectful badinage covered a belief in his powers hardly second even to old Brodribb's. I was, in fact, almost prepared to discover that those preposterous blood-films had, after all, yielded some "illuminating fact" which had sent him hurrying down to Southaven in search of corroboration.

When I alighted from the train on the following day at a little past noon, I found him waiting on the platform, ready to conduct me to his hotel for an early lunch.

"All goes well, so far," he reported. "I attended the post-mortem, and examined the wound thoroughly. The pistol was held in the right hand not more than two inches from the head; probably quite close, for the skin is scorched and heavily tattooed with black powder grains. I find that Riggs was right-handed. So the prima facie probabilities are in favour of suicide; and the recent loss of money suggests a reasonable motive."

"But what about that blood in the hall?"

"Oh, we have disposed of that. I completed the blood-film series last night."

I looked at him quickly to see if he was serious or only playing a facetious return-shot. But his face was as a face of wood.

"You are an exasperating old devil, Thorndyke!" I exclaimed with conviction. Then, knowing that cross-examination would be futile, I asked: "What are we going to do after lunch?"

"The inspector is going to show us over 'the scene of the tragedy,' as the newspapers would express it."

I noted gratefully that he had reserved this item for me, and dismissed professional topics for the time being, concentrating my attention on the old-world, amphibious streets through which we were walking. There is always something interesting in the aspect of a sea-port town, even if it is only a small one like Southaven.

The inspector arrived with such punctuality that he found us still at the table and was easily induced to join us with a cup of coffee and to accept a cigar – administered by Thorndyke, as I suspected, with the object of hindering conversation. I could see that his interest in my colleague was intense and not unmingled with awe, a fact which, in conjunction with the cigar, restrained him from any undue manifestations of curiosity, but not from continuous, though furtive, observation of my friend. Indeed, when we arrived at the late Mr. Riggs's house, I was secretly amused by the close watch that he kept on Thorndyke's movements, unsensational as the inspection turned out to be.

The house, itself, presented very little of interest excepting its picturesque old-world exterior, which fronted on a quiet by-street and was furnished with a deep bay which, as Thorndyke ascertained, commanded a clear view of the street from end to end. It was a rather shabby, neglected little house, as might have been expected, and our examination of it yielded, so far as I could see, only a single fact of any significance: which was that there appeared to be no connection what ever between

89

the blood-stain on the study floor and the train of large spots from the middle of the hall to the street door. And on this piece of evidence – definitely unfavourable from our point of view – Thorndyke concentrated his attention when he had made a preliminary survey.

Closely followed by the watchful inspector, he browsed round the little room, studying every inch of the floor between the blood-stain and the door. The latter he examined minutely from top to bottom, especially as to the handle, the jambs, and the lintel. Then he went out into the hall, scrutinising the floor inch by inch, poring over the walls, and even looking behind the framed prints that hung on them. A reflector lamp suspended by a nail on the wall received minute and prolonged attention, as did also a massive lamp-hook screwed into one of the beams of the low ceiling, of which Thorndyke remarked as he stooped to pass under it, that it must have been fixed there by a dwarf.

"Yes," the inspector agreed, "and a fool. A swinging lamp hung on that hook would have blocked the whole fairway. There isn't too much room as it is. What a pity we weren't a bit more careful about footprints in this place. There are plenty of tracks of wet feet here on this oil-cloth; faint, but you could have made them out all right if they hadn't been all on top of one another. There's Mr. Foxley's, the girl's, mine, and the men who carried out the body, but I'm hanged if I can tell which is which. It's a regular mix up."

"Yes," I agreed, "it is all very confused. But I notice one rather odd thing. There are several faint traces of a large right foot, but I can't see any sign of the corresponding left foot. Can you?"

"Perhaps this is it," said Thorndyke, pointing to a large, vague oval mark. "I have noticed that it seems to occur in some sort of connection with the big right foot; but I must admit that it is not a very obvious foot-print."

"I shouldn't have taken it for a foot-print at all, or at any rate, not a human foot-print. It is more like the spoor of some big animal."

"It is," Thorndyke agreed; "but whatever it is, it seems to have been here before any of the others arrived. You notice that wherever it occurs, it seems to have been trodden on by some of the others."

"Yes, I had noticed that, and the same is true of the big right foot, so it seems probable that they are connected, as you say. But I am hanged if I can make anything of it. Can you, inspector?"

The inspector shook his head. He could not recognise the mark as a foot-print, but he could see very plainly that he had been a fool not to have taken more care to protect the floor.

When the examination of the hall was finished, Thorndyke opened the door and looked at the big, flat doorstep. "What was the weather like here on Wednesday evening?" he asked.

"Showery," the inspector replied; "and there were one or two heavy showers during the night. You were noticing that there are no blood-tracks on the doorstep. But there wouldn't be in any case; for if a man had come out of this door dropping blood, the blood would have dropped on wet stone and got washed away at once."

Thorndyke admitted the truth of this; and so another item of favourable evidence was extinguished. The probability that the blood in the hall was that of some person other than the deceased remained undisturbed; and I could not see that a single fact had been elicited by our inspection of the house that was in any way helpful to our client. Indeed, it appeared to me that there was absolutely no case for the defence, and I even asked myself whether we were not, in fact, merely trying to fudge up a defence for an obviously guilty man. It was not like Thorndyke to do that. But how did the case stand? There was a suggestion of suicide, but a clear possibility of homicide. There was strong evidence that a second person had been in the house, and that person appeared to have received a wound. But a wound suggested a struggle; and the servant's evidence was to the effect that when she left the house a violent altercation was in progress. The deceased was never again seen alive; and the other party to the quarrel bad been found with property of the dead man in his possession. Moreover, there was a clear motive for the crime, stupid as that crime was. For the dead man had threatened to revoke his will but as he had presumably not done so, his death left the will still operative. In short, everything pointed to the guilt of our client, Robert Fletcher.

I had just reached this not very gratifying conclusion when a statement of Thorndyke's shattered my elaborate summing up into impalpable fragments.

"I suppose, sir," said the inspector, "there isn't anything that you would care to tell us, as you are for the defence. But we are not hostile to Fletcher. In fact, he hasn't been charged. He is only being detained in custody until we have heard what turns up at the inquest. I know you have examined that blood that Mr. Foxley took, and Fletcher's blood, too, and you've seen the premises. We have given all the facilities that we could, and if you could give us any sort of hint that might be useful, I should be very much obliged."

Thorndyke reflected for a few moments. Then he replied: "There is no reason for secrecy in regard to you, inspector, who have been so helpful and friendly, so I will be quite frank. I have examined both samples of blood and Fletcher's, and I have inspected the premises; and what I am able to say definitely is this: the blood in the hall is not the blood of the deceased–"

"Ah!" exclaimed the inspector, " I was afraid it wasn't."

"And it is not the blood of Robert Fletcher."

"Isn't it now! Well, I am glad to hear that."

"Moreover," continued Thorndyke, "it was shed well after nine o'clock at night, probably not earlier than midnight."

"There, now!" the inspector exclaimed, with an admiring glance at Thorndyke, "just think of that. See what it is to be a man of science! I suppose, sir, you couldn't give us any sort of description of the person who dropped that blood in the hall?"

Staggered as I had been by Thorndyke's astonishing statements, I could not repress a grin at the inspector's artless question. But the grin faded rather abruptly as Thorndyke replied in matter-of-fact tones: "A detailed description is, of course, impossible. I can only sketch out the probabilities. But if you should happen to meet with a negro – a tall negro with a bandaged head or a contused wound of the scalp and a swollen leg – you had better keep your eye on him. The leg which is swollen is probably the left."

The inspector was thrilled; and so was I, for that matter. The thing was incredible; but yet I knew that Thorndyke's amazing deductions were the products of perfectly orthodox scientific methods. Only I could form no sort of guess as to how they had been arrived at. A negro's blood is no different from any other person's, and certainly affords no clue to his height or the condition of his legs. I could make nothing of it: and as the dialogue and the inspector's note-takings brought us to the little town hall in which the inquest was to be held, I dismissed the puzzle until such time as Thorndyke chose to solve it.

When we entered the town hall we found everything in readiness for the opening of the proceedings. The jury were already in their places and the coroner was just about to take his seat at the head of the long table. We accordingly slipped on to the two chairs that were found for us by the inspector, and the latter took his place behind the jury and facing us. Near to him Mr. Foxley and Miss Markham were seated, and evidently hailed our arrival with profound relief, each of them smiling us a silent greeting. A professional-looking man sitting next to Thorndyke I assumed to be the medical witness, and a rather good young man who sat apart with a police constable I identified as Robert Fletcher.

The evidence of the "common" witnesses, who deposed to the general facts, told us nothing that we did not already know, excepting that it was made clear that Fletcher had left his uncle's house not later than seven o'clock and that thereafter until the following morning his whereabouts were known. The medical witness was cautious, and kept an uneasy eye on Thorndyke. The wound which caused the death of deceased might have been inflicted by himself or by some other person. He had originally given the probable time of death as six or seven o'clock on Wednesday evening. He now admitted reply to a question from Thorndyke that he had not taken the temperature of the body, and that the rigidity and other conditions were not absolutely inconsistent with a considerable later time of death. Death might even have occurred after midnight.

In spite of this admission, however, the sum of the evidence tended strongly to implicate Fletcher, and one or two questions from jurymen suggested a growing belief in his guilt. I had no doubt whatever that if the case had been put to the jury at this stage, a unanimous verdict of "wilful murder" would have been the result. But, as the medical witness returned to his seat, the coroner fixed an inquisitive eye on Thorndyke.

"You have not been summoned as a witness, Dr. Thorndyke," said he, "but I understand that you have made certain investigations in this case. Are you able to throw any fresh light on the circumstances of the death of the deceased, Joseph Riggs?

"Yes," Thorndyke replied. "I am in a position to give important and material evidence."

Thereupon he was sworn, and the coroner, still watching him curiously, said: "I am informed that you have examined samples of the blood of deceased and the blood which was found in the hall of deceased's house. Did you examine them, and if so, what was the object of the examination?"

"I examined both samples and also samples of the blood of Robert Fletcher. The object was to ascertain whether the blood on the hall floor was the blood of the deceased or of Robert Fletcher."

The coroner glanced at the medical witness, and a faint smile appeared on the face of each.

"And did you," the former asked in a slightly ironical tone, "form any opinion on the subject?"

"I ascertained definitely that the blood in the hall was neither that of the deceased nor that of Robert Fletcher."

The coroner's eyebrows went up, and once more he glanced significantly at the doctor.

"But," he demanded incredulously, "is it possible to distinguish the blood of one person from that of another?"

"Usually it is not, but in certain exceptional cases it is. This happened to be an exceptional case."

"In what respect?"

"It happened," Thorndyke replied, "that the person whose blood was found in the hall suffered from the parasitic disease known as filariasis. His blood was infested with swarms of a minute worm named *Filaria nocturna*. I have here," he continued, taking out of his research-case the two bottles and the three boxes, "thirty-six mounted specimens of this blood, and in every one of them one or more of the parasites is to be seen. I have also thirty-six mounted specimens each of the blood of the deceased and. the blood of Robert Fletcher. In not one of these specimens is a single parasite to be found. Moreover, I have examined Robert Fletcher and the body of the deceased, and can testify that no sign of filarial disease was to be discovered in either. Hence it is certain, that the blood found in the halt was not the blood of either of these two persons."

The ironic smile had faded from the coroner's face. He was evidently deeply impressed, and his manner was quite deferential as he asked: "Do these very remarkable observations of yours lead to any further inferences?"

"Yes," replied Thorndyke. "They render it certain that this blood was shed no earlier than nine o'clock and probably nearer midnight."

"Really!" the astonished coroner exclaimed. "Now, how is it possible to fix the time in that exact manner?"

"By inference from the habits of the parasite," Thorndyke explained. "This particular *filaria* is distributed by the mosquito, and its habits are adapted to the habits of the mosquito. During the day, the worms are not found in the blood; they remain hidden in the tissues of the body. But about nine o'clock at night they begin to migrate from the tissues into the blood, and remain in the blood during the hours when the mosquitoes are active. Then about six o'clock in the morning, they leave the blood and migrate back into the tissues.

"There is another very similar species – *Filaria diurna* – which has exactly opposite habits, adapted to day-flying suctorial insects. It appears in the blood about eleven in the forenoon and goes back into the tissues at about six o'clock in the evening."

"Astonishing!" exclaimed the coroner. "Wonderful! By the way, the parasites that you found could not, I suppose, have been *Filaria diurna*?"

"No," Thorndyke replied. "The time excludes that possibility. The blood was certainly shed after six. They were undoubtedly nocturna, and the large numbers found suggest a late hour. The parasites come out of the tissues very gradually, and it is only about midnight that they appear in the blood in really large numbers."

"That is very important," said the coroner. "But does this disease affect any particular class of persons?"

"Yes," Thorndyke replied. "As the disease is con fined to tropical countries, the sufferers are naturally residents of the tropics, and nearly always natives. In West Africa, for instance, it is common among the negroes but practically unknown among the white residents."

"Should you say that there is a distinct probability that this unknown person was a negro?"

"Yes. But apart from the *filaria* there is direct evidence that he was. Searching for some cause of the bleeding, I noticed a lamp-hook screwed into the ceiling, and low enough to strike a tall man's head. I examined it closely, and observed on it a dark, shiny mark, like a blood-smear, and one or two short coiled hairs which I recognised as the scalp-hairs of a negro. I have no doubt that the unknown man is a negro, and that he has a wound of the scalp."

"Does filarial disease produce any effects that can be recognised?

"Frequently it does. One of the commonest effects produced by *Filaria nocturna*, especially among negroes, is the condition known as elephantiasis. This consists of an enormous swelling of the extremities, most usually of one leg, including the foot; whence the name. The leg and foot look like those of an elephant. As a matter of fact, the negro who was in the hall suffered from elephantiasis of the left leg. I observed prints of the characteristically deformed foot on the oil-cloth covering the floor."

Thorndyke's evidence was listened to with intense interest by everyone present, including myself. Indeed, so spell-bound was his audience that one could have heard a pin drop; and the breathless silence continued for some seconds after he had ceased speaking. Then, in the midst of the stillness, I heard the door creak softly behind me.

There was nothing particularly significant in the sound. But its effects were amazing. Glancing at the inspector, who faced the door, I saw his eyes open and his jaw drop until his face was a very mask of astonishment. And as this expression was reflected on the faces of the jurymen, the coroner and everyone present, excepting Thorndyke, whose back was towards the door, I turned to see what had happened. And then I was as astonished as the others.

The door had been pushed open a few inches and a head thrust in – a negro's head, covered with a soiled and blood rag forming a rough bandage. As I gazed at the black, shiny, inquisitive face, the man pushed the door farther open and shuffled into the room; and instantly there arose on all sides a soft rustle and an inarticulate murmur followed by breathless silence, while every eye was riveted on the man's left leg.

It certainly was a strange, repulsive – looking member, its monstrous bulk exposed to view through the slit trouser and its great shapeless foot – shoeless, since no shoe could have contained it – rough and horny like the foot of an elephant. But it was tragic and pitiable, too for the man, apart from this horrible excrescence, was a fine, big, athletic-looking fellow.

The coroner was the first to recover. Addressing Thorndyke, but keeping an eye on the negro, he said: "Your evidence, then, amounts to this: On the night of Joseph Riggs' death, there was a stranger in the house. That stranger was a negro, who seems to have wounded his head and who, you say, had a swelled left leg."

"Yes," Thorndyke admitted, "that is the substance of my evidence."

Once more a hush fell on the room. The negro stood near the door, rolling his eyes to and fro over the assembly as if uneasily conscious that everyone was looking at him. Suddenly, he shuffled up to the foot of the table and addressed the coroner in deep, buzzing, resonant tones. "You tink I kill dat ole man! I no kill um. He kill himself. I look um."

Having made this statement, he rolled his eyes defiantly round the court, and then turned his face expectantly towards the coroner, who said: "You say you know that Mr. Riggs killed himself?"

"Yas. I look um. He shoot himself. You tink I shoot urn. I tell you I no shoot um. Why I fit kill this man? I no sabby um."

"Then," said the coroner, "if you know that he killed himself, you must tell us all that you know; and you must swear to tell us the truth."

"Yas," the negro agreed, "I tell you eberyting one time. I tell you de troof. Dat ole man kill himself."

When the coroner had explained to him that he was not bound to make any statement that would incriminate him, as he still elected to give evidence, he was sworn and proceeded to make his statement with curious fluency and self-possession.

"My name Robert Bruce. Dat my English name. My country name Kwaku Mensab. I live for Winnebah on de Gold Coast. Dis time I cook's mate for dat steamer Leckie. On Wednesday night I lay in my bunk. I no fit sleep. My leg he chook me. I look out of de porthole. Plenty moon live. In my country when de moon big, peoples walk about. So I get up. I go ashore to walk about de town. Den de rain come. Plenty rain. Rain no good for my sickness. So I try for open house doors. No fit. All doors locked. Den I come to dis ole man's house. I turn de handle. De door open. I go in. I look in one room. All dark. Nobody live. Den I look annudder room. De door open a little. Light live inside. I no like dat I tink, spose somebody come out and see me, be link I come for teef someting. So I tink I go away.

"Den someting make 'Ping!' same like gun. I hear someting fail down in dat room. I go to de door and I sing out, 'Who live in dere?' Nobody say nutting. So I open de door and look in. De room full ob smoke. I look dat ale man on de floor. I look dat pistol. I sabby dat ole man kill himself. Den I frighten

99

too much. I run out. D place all dark. Someting knock my head. He make blood come plenty. I go back for ship. I no say nutting to nobody. Dis day I hear peoples talk 'bout dis inquess to find out who kill dat ole man. So I come to hear what peoples say. I hear dat gentleman say I kill dat ole man. So I tell you eberyting. I tell you de troof. Finish."

"Do you know what time it was when you came ashore?" the coroner asked.

"Yas. When I come down de ladder I hear eight bells ring. I get back to de ship jus' before dey ring two bells in de middle watch."

"Then you came ashore at midnight and got back just before one o'clock?"

"Yas. Dat is what I say."

A few more questions put by the coroner having elicited nothing fresh, the case was put briefly to the jury.

"You have heard the evidence, gentlemen, and most remarkable evidence it was. Like myself, you must have been deeply impressed by the amazing skill with which Dr. Thorndyke reconstructed the personality of the unknown visitor to that house, and even indicated correctly the very time of the visit, from an examination of a mere chance blood-stain. As to the statement of Kwaku Mensab, I can only say that I see no reason to doubt its truth. You will note that it is in complete agreement with Dr. Thorndyke's evidence, and it presents no inconsistencies or improbabilities. Possibly the police may wish to make some further inquiries, but for our purposes it is the evidence of an eyewitness, and as such must be given full weight. With these remarks, I leave you to consider your verdict."

The jury took but a minute or two to deliberate. Indeed, only one verdict was possible if the evidence was to be accepted, and that was agreed on unanimously – suicide whilst temporarily insane. As soon as it was announced, the inspector, formally and with congratulations, released Fletcher from custody, and presently retired in company with the negro to make a few inquiries on board the ship.

The rising of the court was the signal for a wild demonstration of enthusiasm and gratitude to Thorndyke. To play his part efficiently in that scene he would have needed to be furnished, like certain repulsive Indian deities, with an unlimited outfit of arms. For everyone wanted to shake his hand, and two of them – Mr. Foxley and Miss Markham – did so with such pertinacity as entirely to exclude the other candidates.

"I can never thank you enough," Miss Markham exclaimed, with swimming eyes, "if I should live to be a hundred. But I shall think of you with gratitude every day of my life. Whenever I look at Robert, I shall remember that his liberty, and even his life, are your gifts."

Here she was so overcome by grateful emotion that she again seized and pressed his hand. I think she was within an ace of kissing him; but being, perhaps, doubtful how he would take it, compromised by kissing Robert instead. And, no doubt, it was just as well.

The Touchstone

It happened not uncommonly that the exigencies of practice committed my friend Thorndyke to investigations that lay more properly within the province of the police. For problems that had arisen as secondary consequences of a criminal act could usually not be solved until the circumstances of that act were fully elucidated and, incidentally, the identity of the actor established. Such a problem was that of the disappearance of James Harewood's will, a problem that was propounded to us by our old friend, Mr. Marchmont, when he called on us, by appointment, with the client of whom he had spoken in his note.

It was just four o'clock when the solicitor arrived at our chambers, and as I admitted him he ushered in a gentlemanly-looking man of about thirty-five, whom he introduced as Mr. William Crowhurst.

"I will just stay," said he with an approving glance at the tea-service on the table, "and have a cup of tea with you, and give you an outline of the case. Then I must run away and leave Mr. Crowhurst to fill in the details."

He seated himself in an easy chair within comfortable reach of the table, and as Thorndyke poured out the tea, he glanced over a few notes scribbled on a sheet of paper.

"I may say," he began, stirring his tea thoughtfully, "that this is a forlorn hope. I have brought the case to you, but I have not the slightest expectation that you will be able to help us."

"A very wholesome frame of mind," Thorndyke commented with a smile. "I hope it is that of your client also."

It is indeed," said Mr. Crowhurst; " in fact, it seems to me a waste of your time to go into the matter. Probably you will think so too, when you have heard the particulars."

"Well, let us hear the particulars," said Thorndyke. "A forlorn hope has, at least, the stimulating quality of difficulty. Let us have your outline sketch, Marchmont."

The solicitor, having emptied his cup and pushed it towards the tray for replenishment, glanced at his notes and began: "The simplest way in which to present the problem is to give a brief recital of the events that have given rise to it, which are these: The day before yesterday – that is last Monday – at a quarter to two in the afternoon, Mr. James Harewood executed a will at his house at Merbridge, which is about two miles from Welsbury. There were present four persons: two of his servants, who signed as witnesses, and the two principal beneficiaries – Mr. Arthur Baxfield, a nephew of the testator, and our friend here, Mr. William Crowhurst. The will was a holograph written on the two pages of a sheet of letter-paper. When the witnesses signed, the will was covered by another sheet of paper so that only the space for the signatures was exposed. Neither of the witnesses read the will, nor did either of the beneficiaries; and so far as I am aware, no one but the testator knew what were its actual provisions, though, after the servants had left the room, Mr. Harewood explained its general purport to the beneficiaries."

"And what was its general purport?" Thorndyke asked.

"Broadly speaking," replied Marchmont, "it divided the estate in two very unequal portions between Mr. Baxfield and Mr. Crowhurst. There were certain small legacies of which neither the amounts nor the names of the legatees are known. Then, to Baxfield was given a thousand pounds to enable him either to buy a partnership or to start a small factory – he is a felt hat manufacturer by trade – and the remainder to Crowhurst, who was made executor and residuary legatee. But, of course, the residue of the estate is an unknown quantity, since we don't know either the number or the amounts of the legacies.

"Shortly after the signing of the will, the parties separated. Mr. Harewood folded up the will and put it in a leather wallet which he slipped into his pocket, stating his intention of taking the will forthwith to deposit with his lawyer at Welsbury. A few minutes after his guests had departed, he was seen by one of the servants to leave the house, and afterwards was seen by a neighbour walking along a footpath which, after passing through a small wood, joins the main road about a mile and a quarter from Welsbury. From that time, he was never again seen alive. He never visited the lawyer, nor did anyone see him at or near Welsbury or elsewhere else.

"As he did not return home that night, his housekeeper (he was a widower and childless) became extremely alarmed, and in the morning she communicated with the police. A search-party was organised, and, following the path on which he was last seen, explored the wood – which is known as Gilbert's Copse – and here, at the bottom of an old chalk-pit, they found him lying dead with a fractured skull and a dislocated neck. How he came by these injuries is not at present known; but as the body had been robbed of all valuables, including his watch, purse, diamond ring and the wallet containing the will, there is naturally a strong suspicion that he has been murdered. That, however, is not our immediate concern – at least not mine. I am concerned with the will, which, as you see, has disappeared, and as it has presumably been carried away by a thief who is under suspicion of murder, it is not likely to be returned."

"It is almost certainly destroyed by this time," said Mr. Crowhurst.

"That certainly seems probable," Thorndyke agreed. "But what do you want me to do? You haven't come for counsel's opinion?"

"No," replied Marchmont. "I am pretty clear about the legal position. I shall claim, as the will has presumably been destroyed, to have the testator's wishes carried out in so far as they are known. But I am doubtful as to the view the court may take. It may decide that the testator's wishes are not known, that the provisions of the will are too uncertain to admit of administration."

"And what would be the effect of that decision?" asked Thorndyke.

"In that case," said Marchmont, "the entire estate would go to Baxfield, as he is the next of kin and there was no previous will."

"And what is it that you want me to do?"

Marchmont chuckled deprecatingly. "You have to pay the penalty of being a prodigy, Thorndyke. We are asking you to do an impossibility – but we don't really expect you to bring it off. We ask you to help us to recover the will."

"If the will has been completely destroyed, it can't be recovered," said Thorndyke. "But we don't know that it has been destroyed. The matter is, at least, worth investigating; and if you wish me to look into it, I will."

The solicitor rose with an air of evident relief.

"Thank you, Thorndyke," said he. "I expect nothing – at least, I tell myself that I do – but I can now feel that everything that is possible will be done. And now I must be off. Crowhurst can give you any details that you want."

When Marchmont had gone, Thorndyke turned to our client and asked, "What do you suppose Baxfield will do, if the will is irretrievably lost? Will he press his claim as next of kin?"

"I should say yes," replied Crowhurst. "He is a business man and his natural claims are greater than mine. He is not likely to refuse what the law assigns to him as his right. As a matter of fact, I think he felt that his uncle had treated him unfairly in alienating the property."

"Was there any reason for this diversion of the estate?"

"Well," replied Crowhurst, "Harewood and I have been very good friends and he was under some obligations to me; and then Baxfield had not made himself very acceptable to his uncle. But the principal factor, I think, was a strong tendency of Baxfield's to gamble. He had lost quite a lot of money by backing horses, and a careful, thrifty man like James Harewood doesn't care to leave his savings to a gambler. The thousand pounds that he did leave to Baxfield was expressly for the purpose of investment in a business."

"Is Baxfield in business now?"

"Not on his own account. He is a sort of foreman or shop-manager in a factory just outside Welsbury, and I believe he is a good worker and knows his trade thoroughly."

"And now," said Thorndyke, "with regard to Mr Harewood's death. The injuries might, apparently, have been either accidental or homicidal. What are the probabilities of accident – disregarding the robbery?

"Very considerable, I should say. It is a most dangerous place. The footpath runs close beside the edge of a disused chalk-pit with perpendicular or over hanging sides, and the edge is masked by bushes and brambles. A careless walker might easily fall over – or be pushed over, for that matter."

"Do you know when the inquest is to take place?"

"Yes. The day after to-morrow. I had the subpoena this morning for Friday afternoon at 2.30, at the Welsbury Town Hall."

At this moment footsteps were heard hurriedly ascending the stairs and then came a loud and peremptory rat-tat at our door. I sprang across to see who our visitor was, and as I flung open the door, Mr. Marchmont rushed in, breathing heavily and flourishing a newspaper.

"Here is a new development," he exclaimed. "It doesn't seem to help us much, but I thought you had better know about it at once." He sat down, and putting on his spectacles, read aloud as follows: "A new and curious light has been thrown on the mystery of the death of Mr. James Harewood, whose body was found yesterday in a disused chalk-pit near Merbridge. It appears that on Monday – the day on which Mr. Harewood almost certainly was killed – a passenger alighting from a train at Barwood Junction before it had stopped, slipped and fell between the train and the platform. He was quickly extricated, and as he had evidently sustained internal injuries, he was taken to the local hospital, where he was found to be suffering from a fractured pelvis. He gave his name as Thomas Fletcher, but refused to give any address, saying that he had no relatives. This morning he died, and on his clothes being searched for an address, a parcel, formed of two handkerchiefs tied up with string, was found in his pocket. When it was opened it was found to contain five watches, three watch-chains, a tie-pin and a number of bank-notes. Other pockets contained a quantity of loose money – gold and silver mixed – and a card of the Welsbury Races, which were held on Monday. Of the five watches, one has been identified as the one taken from Mr. Harewood; and the bank-notes have been identified as a batch handed to him by the cashier, of his bank at Welsbury last Thursday and presumably carried in the leather wallet which was stolen from his pocket. This wallet, by the way, has also been found. It was picked up – empty – last night on the railway embankment just outside Welsbury Station. Appearances thus suggest that the man, Fletcher, when on his way to the races, encountered Mr. Harewood in the lonely copse, and murdered and robbed him; or perhaps found him dead in the chalk-pit and robbed the body – a question that is now never likely to be solved."

As Marchmont finished reading, he looked up at Thorndyke. "It doesn't help us much, does it?" said he. "As the wallet was found empty, it is pretty certain that the will has been destroyed."

"Or perhaps merely thrown away," said Thorndyke. "In which case an advertisement offering a substantial reward may bring it to light."

The solicitor shrugged his shoulders sceptically, but agreed to publish the advertisement. Then, once more he turned to go; and as Mr. Crowhurst had no further information to give, he departed with his lawyer.

For some time after they had gone, Thorndyke sat with his brief notes before him, silent and deeply reflective. I, too, maintained a discreet silence, for I knew from long experience that the motionless pose and quiet, impassive face were the outward signs of a mind in swift and strenuous action. Instinctively, I gathered that this apparently chaotic case was being quietly sorted out and arranged in a logical order; that Thorndyke, like a skilful chess-player, was "trying over the moves" before he should lay his hand upon the pieces.

Presently he looked up. "Well?" he asked. "What do you think, Jervis? Is it worth while?"

"That," I replied," depends on whether the will is or is not in existence. If it has been destroyed, an investigation would be a waste of our time and our client's money."

"Yes," he agreed. "But there is quite a good chance that it has not been destroyed. It was probably dropped loose into the wallet, and then might have been picked out and thrown away before the wallet was examined. But we mustn't concentrate too much on the will. If we take up the case – which I am inclined to do – we must ascertain the actual sequence of events. We have one clear day before the inquest. If we run down to Merbridge to-morrow and go thoroughly over the ground, and then go on to Barwood and find out all we can about the man

Fletcher, we may get some new light from the evidence at the inquest."

I agreed readily to Thorndyke's proposal, not that I could see any way into the case, but I felt a conviction that my colleague had isolated some leading fact and had a definite line of research in his mind. And this conviction deepened when, later in the evening, he laid his research-case on the table, and rearranged its contents with evident purpose. I watched curiously the apparatus that he was packing in it and tried – not very successfully – to infer the nature of the proposed investigation. The box of powdered paraffin wax and the spirit blowpipe were obvious enough; but the "dust-aspirator" – a sort of miniature vacuum cleaner – the portable microscope, the coil of Manila line, with an eye spliced into one end, and especially the abundance of blank-labelled microscope slides, all of which I saw him pack in the case with deliberate care, defeated me utterly.

About ten o'clock on the following morning we stepped from the train in Welsbury Station, and having recovered our bicycles from the luggage van, wheeled them through the barrier and mounted. During the train journey we had both studied the one-inch Ordnance map to such purpose that we were virtually in familiar surroundings and immune from the necessity of seeking directions from the natives. As we cleared the town we glanced up the broad by-road to the left which led to the race-course; then we rode on briskly for a mile, which brought us to the spot where the footpath to Merbridge joined the road. Here we dismounted and, lifting our bicycles over the stile, followed the path towards a small wood which we could see ahead, crowning a low hill.

"For such a good path," Thorndyke remarked as we approached the wood, "it is singularly unfrequented. I haven't seen a soul since we left the road." He glanced at the map as the path entered the wood, and when we had walked on a couple of hundred yards, he halted and stood his bicycle against a tree.

"The chalk-pit should be about here," said he, "though it is impossible to see. He grasped a stem of one of the small bushes that crowded on to the path and pulled it aside. Then he uttered an exclamation.

"Just look at that, Jervis. It is a positive scandal that a public path should be left in this condition."

Certainly Mr. Crowhurst had not exaggerated. It was a most dangerous place. The parted branches revealed a chasm some thirty feet deep, the brink of which, masked by the bushes, was but a matter of inches from the edge of the path.

"We had better go back," said Thorndyke," and find the entrance to the pit, which seems to be to the right. The first thing is to ascertain exactly where Harewood fell. Then we can come back and examine the place from above."

We turned back, and presently found a faint track which we followed until, descending steeply, it brought us out into the middle of the pit. It was evidently an ancient pit, for the sides were blackened by age, and the floor was occupied by a trees, some of considerable size. Against one of these we leaned our bicycles and then walked slowly round at the foot of the frowning cliff.

"This seems to be below the path," said Thorndyke, glancing up at the grey wall which jutted out above in stages like an inverted flight of steps. "Somewhere hereabouts we should find some traces of the tragedy."

Even as he spoke my eye caught a spot of white on a block of chalk, and on the freshly fractured surface a significant brownish-red stain. The block lay opposite the mouth of an artificial cave – an old wagon-shelter but now empty and immediately under a markedly overhanging part of the cliff.

"This is undoubtedly the place where he fell," said Thorndyke. "You can see where the stretcher was placed – an old-pattern stretcher with wheel-runners – and there is a little spot of broken soil at the top where he came over. Well, apart from the robbery, a clear fall of over thirty feet is enough to account for a fractured skull. Will you stay here, Jervis, while I run up and look at the path?"

He went off towards the entrance, and presently I heard him above, pulling aside the bushes, and after one or two trials, he appeared directly overhead.

"There are plenty of footprints on the path," said he, "but nothing abnormal. No trampling or signs of a struggle. I am going on a little farther."

He withdrew behind the bushes, and I proceeded to inspect the interior of the cave, noting the smoke-blackened roof and the remains of a recent fire, which, with a number of rabbit bones and a discarded tea of the kind used by the professional tramp, seemed not without a possible bearing on our investigation. I was thus engaged when I heard Thorndyke hail me from above and coming out of the cave, I saw his head thrust between the branches. He seemed to be lying down, for his face was nearly on a level with the top of the cliff.

"I want to take an impression," he called out. "Will you bring up the paraffin and the blower? And you might bring the coil of line, too."

I hurried away to the place where our bicycles were standing, and opening the research-case, took out the coil of line, the tin of paraffin wax and the spirit blowpipe, and having ascertained that the container of the latter was full, I ran up the incline and made my way along the path. Some distance along, I found my colleague nearly hidden in the bushes, lying prone, with his head over the edge of the cliff.

"You see, Jervis," he said, as I crawled alongside and looked over, "this is a possible way down, and someone has used it quite recently. He climbed down with his face to the cliff – you can see the clear impression of the toe of a boot in the loam of that projection, and you can even make out the shape of an iron toe-tip. Now the problem is how to get down to take the impression without, dislodging the earth above it. I think I will secure myself with the line."

"It is hardly worth the risk of a broken neck," said I. "Probably the print is that of some schoolboy."

"It is a man's foot," he replied. "Most likely it has no connection with our case. But it may have, and as a shower of rain would obliterate it we ought to secure it." As he spoke, he passed the end of the cord through eye and slipped the loop over his shoulders, drawing tight under his arms. Then, having made the line fast to the butt of a small tree, he cautiously lowered himself over the edge and climbed down to the projection. A soon as he had a secure footing, I passed the spare cord through the ring on the lid of the wax tin and lowered it to him, and when he had unfastened it, I drew up the cord and in the same way let down the blowpipe. Then I watched his neat, methodical procedure. First he took out a spoonful of the powdered, or grated, wax and very delicately sprinkled it on the toe-print until the latter was evenly but very thinly covered. Next he lit the blowlamp, and as soon as the blue flame began to roar from the pipe, he directed it on to the toe-print. Almost instantly the powder melted, glazing the impression like a coat of varnish. The flame was removed and the film of wax at once solidified and became dull and opaque. A second, heavier, sprinkling with the powder, followed by another application of the flame, thickened the film of wax, and this process, repeated four or five times, eventually produced a solid cake. Then Thorndyke extinguished the blowlamp, and securing it and the tin to the cord, directed me to pull them up. "And you might send me down the field-glasses," he added. "There is something farther down that I can't quite make out."

I slipped the glasses from my shoulder, and opening the case, tied the cord to the leather sling and lowered it down the cliff; and then I watched with some curiosity as Thorndyke stood on his insecure perch steadily gazing through the glasses (they were Zeiss 8-prismatics) at a clump of wallflowers that grew from a boss of chalk about half-way down. Presently he lowered the glasses and, slinging them round his neck by their lanyard, turned his attention to the cake of wax. It was by this time quite solid, and when he had tested it, he lifted it carefully, and placed it in the empty binocular case, when I drew it up.

"I want you, Jervis," Thorndyke called up, "to steady the line. I am going down to that wallflower clump."

It looked extremely unsafe, but I knew it was useless to protest, so I hitched the line around a massive stump and took a firm grip of the "fall."

"Ready," I sang out; and forthwith Thorndyke began to creep across the face of the cliff with feet and hands clinging to almost invisible projections. Fortunately, there was at this part no overhang, and though my heart was in my mouth as I watched, I saw him cross the perilous space in safety. Arrived at the clump, he drew an envelope from his pocket, stooped and picked up some small object, which he placed in the envelope, returning the latter to his pocket. Then he gave me another bad five minutes while he recrossed the nearly vertical surface to his starting-point; but at length this, too, was safely accomplished, and when he finally climbed up over the edge and stood beside me on solid earth, I drew a deep breath and turned to revile him.

"Well?" I demanded sarcastically, "what have you gathered at the risk of your neck? Is it samphire or edelweiss?"

He drew the envelope from his pocket, and dipping into it, produced a cigarette-holder – a cheap bone affair, black and clammy with long service and still holding the butt of a hand-made cigarette – and handed it to me. I turned it over, smelled it and hastily handed it back. "For my part," said I, "I wouldn't have risked the cervical vertebra of a yellow cat for it. What do you expect to learn from it?"

"Of course, I expect nothing. We are just collecting facts on the chance that they may turn out to be relevant. Here, for instance, we find that a man has descended, within a few yards of where Harewood fell, by this very inconvenient route, instead of going round to the entrance to the pit. He must have had some reason for adopting this undesirable mode of descent. Possibly he was in a hurry, and probably he belonged to the district, since a stranger would not know of the existence of this short cut. Then it seems likely that this was his cigarette tube. If you look over, you will see by those vertical scrapes on the chalk that he slipped and must have nearly fallen. At that moment he probably dropped the tube, for you notice that the wallflower clump is directly under the marks of his toes."

"Why do you suppose he did not recover the tube?"

"Because the descent slopes away from the position of the clump, and he had no trusty Jervis with a stout cord to help him to cross the space. And if he went down this way because he was hurried, he would not have time to search for the tube. But if the tube was not his, still it belonged to somebody who has been here recently."

"Is there anything that leads you to connect this man with the crime?"

"Nothing but time and place," he replied. "The man has been down into the pit close to where Harewood was robbed and possibly murdered, and as the traces are quite recent, he must have been there near about the time of the robbery. That is all. I am considering the traces of this man in particular because there are no traces of any other. But we may as well have a look at the path, which, as you see, yields good impressions."

We walked slowly along the path towards Merbridge, keeping at the edges and scrutinising the surface closely. In the shady hollows, the soft loam bore prints of many feet, and among them we could distinguish one with an iron toe-tip, but it was nearly obliterated by another studded with hob-nails.

"We shan't get much information here," said Thorndyke as he turned about. "The search-party have trodden out the important prints. Let us see if we can find out where the man with the toe-tips went to."

We searched the path on the Welsbury side of the chalk-pit, but found no trace of him. Then we went into the pit, and having located the place where he descended, sought for some other exit than the track leading to the path. Presently, half-way up the slope, we found a second track, bearing away in the direction of Merbridge. Following this for some distance, we came to a small hollow at the bottom of which was a muddy space. And here we both halted abruptly, for in the damp ground were the clear imprints of a pair of boots which we could see had, in addition to the toe-tips, half-tips to the heels.

"We had better have wax casts of these," said Thorndyke, "to compare with the boots of the man Fletcher. I will do them while you go back for the bicycles."

By the time that I returned with the machines two of the footprints were covered with a cake each of wax, and Thorndyke had left the track, and was peering among the bushes. I inquired what he was looking for.

"It is a forlorn hope, as Marchmont would say," he replied, "but I am looking to see if the will has been thrown away here. It was quite probably jettisoned at once, and this is the most probable route for the robber to have taken, if he knew of it. You see by the map that it must lead nearly directly to the race-course, and it avoids both the path and the main road. While the wax is setting we might as well look round."

It seemed a hopeless enough proceeding and I agreed to it without enthusiasm. Leaving the track on the opposite side to that which Thorndyke was searching, I wandered among the bushes and the little open spaces, peering about me and reminding myself of that "aged, aged man" who

"Sometimes searched the grassy knolls,

For wheels of hansom cabs."

I had worked my way nearly back to where I could see Thorndyke, also returning, when my glance fell on a small, brown object caught among the branches of a bush. It was a man's pigskin purse; and as I picked it out of the bush I saw that it was open and empty.

With my prize in my hand, I hastened to the spot where Thorndyke was lifting the wax casts. He looked up and asked, "No luck, I suppose?"

I held out the purse, on which he pounced eagerly. "But this is most important, Jervis," he exclaimed. "It is almost certainly Harewood's purse. You see the initials, 'J. H.,' stamped on the flap. Then we were right as to the direction that the robber took. And it would pay to search this place exhaustively for the will, though we can't do that now, as we have to go to Barwood, I wrote to say we were coming. We had better get back to the path now and make for the road. Barwood is only half-an-hour's run."

We packed the casts in the research-case (which was strapped to Thorndyke's bicycle), and turning back, made our way to the path. As it was still deserted, we ventured to mount, and soon reached the road, along which we started at a good pace toward Barwood.

Half-an-hour's ride brought us into the main Street of the little town, and when we dismounted at the police station we found the Chief Constable himself waiting to receive us, courteously eager to assist us, but possessed by a devouring curiosity which was somewhat inconvenient.

"I have done as you asked me in your letter, sir," he said. "Fletcher's body is, of course, in the mortuary, but I have had all his clothes and effects brought here; and I have had them put in my private office, so that you can look them over in comfort."

"It is exceedingly good of you," said Thorndyke, "and most helpful." He unstrapped the research-case, and following the officer into his sanctum, looked round with deep approval. A large table had been cleared for the examination, and the dead pickpocket's clothes and effects neatly arranged at one end.

Thorndyke's first proceeding was to pick up the dead man's boots – a smart but flimsy pair of light brown leather, rather down at heel and in need of re-soling. Neither toes nor heels bore any tips or even nails excepting the small fastening brads. Having exhibited them to me without remark, Thorndyke placed them on a sheet of white paper and made a careful tracing of the soles, a proceeding that seemed to surprise the Chief Constable, for he remarked, "I should hardly have thought that the question of footprints would arise in this case. You can't charge a dead man."

Thorndyke agreed that this seemed to be true; and then he proceeded to an operation that fairly made the officer's eyes bulge. Opening the research-case – into which the officer cast an inquisitive glance – he took out the dust-aspirator, the nozzle of which he inserted into one after another of the dead thief's pockets while I worked the pump. When he had gone through them all, he opened the receiver and extracted quite a considerable ball of dusty fluff. Placing this on a glass slide, he tore it in halves with a pair of mounted needles and passing one half to me, when we both fell to work "teasing", it out into an open mesh, portions of which we separated and laid – each in a tiny pool of glycerine – on blank labelled glass slides, applying to each slide its cover-glass and writing on the label, "Dust from Fletcher's pockets."

When the series was complete, Thorndyke brought out the microscope, and fitting on a one-inch objective, quickly examined the slides, one after another, and then pushed the microscope to me. So far as I could see, the dust was just ordinary dust – principally made up of broken cotton fibres with a few fibres of wool, linen, wood, jute, and others that I could not name and some undistinguishable mineral particles. But I made no comment, and resigning the microscope to the Chief Constable – who glared through it, breathing hard, and remarked that the dust was "rummy-looking stuff " – watched Thorndyke's further proceedings. And very odd proceedings they were.

First he laid the five stolen watches in a row, and with a Coddington lens minutely examined the dial of each, Then he opened the back of each in turn and copied into his notebook the watch-repairers' scratched inscriptions. Next he produced from the case a number of little vulcanite rods, and laying out five labelled slides, dropped a tiny drop of glycerine on each, covering it at once with a watch-glass to protect it from falling dust. Then he stuck a little label on each watch, wrote a number on it and similarly numbered the five slides. His next proceeding was to take out the glass of watch No. 1 and pick up one of the vulcanite rods, which he rubbed briskly on a silk handkerchief and passed across and around the dial of the watch, after which he held the rod close to the glycerine on slide No. 1 and tapped it sharply with the blade of his pocket-knife. Then he dropped a cover- glass on to the glycerine and made a rapid inspection of the specimen through the microscope.

This operation he repeated on the other four watches, using a fresh rod for each, and when he had finished he turned to the open-mouthed officer. "I take it," said he, "that the watch which has the chain attached to it is Mr. Harewood's watch?"

"Yes, sir. That helped us to identify it." Thorndyke looked at the watch reflectively. Attached to the bow by a short length of green tape was a small, rather elaborate key. This my friend picked up, and taking a fresh mounted needle, inserted it into the barrel of the key, from which he then withdrew it with a tiny ball of fluff on its point. I hastily prepared a slide and handed it to him, when, with a pair of dissecting scissors, he cut off a piece of the fluff and let it fall into the glycerine. He repeated this manoeuvre with two more slides and then labelled the three " Key, outside," "middle" and "inside," and in that order examined them under the microscope.

My own examination of the specimens yielded very little. They all seemed to be common dust, though that from the face of watch No. 3 contained a few broken fragments of what looked like animal hairs – possibly cat's – as also did the key-fluff marked "outside." But if this had any significance, I could not guess what it was. As to the Chief Constable, he clearly looked on the whole proceeding as a sort of legerdemain with no obvious purpose, for he remarked, as we were packing up to go, " I am glad I've seen how you do it, sir. But all the same, I think you are flogging a dead horse. We know who committed the crime and we know he's beyond the reach of the law."

"Well," said Thorndyke, "one must earn one's fee, you know. I shall put Fletcher's boots and the five watches in evidence at the inquest to-morrow, and I will ask you to leave the labels on the watches." With renewed thanks and a hearty handshake he bade the courteous officer adieu, and we rode off to catch the train to London.

That evening, after dinner, we brought out the specimens and went over them at our leisure; and Thorndyke added a further specimen by drawing a knotted piece of twine through the cigarette-holder that he had salved from the chalk-pit, and teasing out the unsavoury, black substance that came out on the string in glycerine on a slide. When he had examined it, he passed it to me, The dark, tarry liquid somewhat obscured the detail, but I could make out fragments of the same animal hairs that I had noted in the other specimens, only here they were much more numerous. I mentioned my observation to Thorndyke. "They are certainly parts of mammalian hairs," I said, "and they look like the hairs of a cat. Are they from a cat?"

"Rabbit," Thorndyke replied curtly; and even then, I am ashamed to admit, I did not perceive the drift of the investigation.

The room in the Welsbury Town Hall had filled up some minutes before the time fixed for the opening of the inquest, and in the interval, when the jury had retired to view the body in the adjacent mortuary, I looked round the assembly. Mr. Marchmont and Mr. Crowhurst were present, and a youngish, horsey-looking man in cord breeches and leggings, whom I correctly guessed to be Arthur Baxfield. Our friend the Chief Constable of Barwood was also there, and with him Thorndyke exchanged a few words in a retired corner. The rest of the company were strangers.

As soon as the coroner and the jury had taken their places the medical witness was called. The cause of death, he stated, was dislocation of the neck, accompanied by a depressed fracture of the skull. The fracture have been produced by a blow with a heavy weapon, or by the deceased falling on his head. The witness adopted the latter view, as the dislocation showed that deceased had fallen in that manner.

The next witness was Mr. Crowhurst, who repeated to the court what he had told us, and further stated that on leaving deceased's house he went straight home, as he had an appointment with a friend. He was followed by Baxfield, who gave evidence to the same effect, and stated that on leaving the house of the deceased he went to his place of business at Welsbury. He was about to retire when Thorndyke rose to cross-examine.

"At what time did you reach your place of business?" he asked.

The witness hesitated for a few moments and then replied, "Half-past four."

"And what time did you leave deceased's house?"

"Two o'clock," was the reply.

"What is the distance?"

"In a direct line, about two miles. But I didn't go direct. I took a round in the country by Lenfield."

"That would take you near the race-course on the way back. Did you go to the races?

"No. The races were just over when I returned."

There was a slight pause and then Thorndyke asked, "Do you smoke much, Mr. Baxfield?"

The witness looked surprised, and so did the jury, but the former replied, "A fair amount. About fifteen cigarettes a day."

"What brand of cigarettes do you smoke, and what kind of tobacco is it?"

"I make my own cigarettes. I make them of shag."

Here protesting murmurs arose from the jury, and the coroner remarked stiffly, "These questions do not appear to have much connection with the subject of this inquiry."

"You may take it, sir," replied Thorndyke, "that they have a very direct bearing on it." Then, turning to the witness he asked, "Do you use a cigarette-tube?

"Sometimes I do," was the reply.

"Have you lost a cigarette-tube lately?"

The witness directed a startled glance at Thorndyke and replied after some hesitation, "I believe I mislaid one a little time ago."

"When and where did you lose that tube?" Thorndyke asked.

"I – I really couldn't say," replied Baxfield, turning perceptibly pale.

Thorndyke opened his dispatch-box, and taking out the tube that he had salved at so much risk, handed it to the witness. "Is that the tube that you lost?" he asked.

At this question Baxfield turned pale as death, and the hand in which he received the tube shook as if with a palsy. "It may be," he faltered. "I wouldn't swear to it. It is like the one I lost."

Thorndyke took it from him and passed it to the coroner. "I am putting this tube in evidence, sir," said he. Then addressing the witness, he said, "You stated that you did not go to the races. Did you go on the course or inside the grounds at all?"

Baxfield moistened his lips and replied, "I just went in for a minute or two, but I didn't stay. The races were over, and there was a very rough crowd."

"While you were in that crowd, Mr Baxfield, did you have your pocket picked?"

There was an expectant silence in the court as Baxfield replied in a low voice: "Yes. I lost my watch."

Again Thorndyke opened the dispatch-box, and taking out a watch (it was the one that had been labelled 3), handed it to the witness. "Is that the watch that you lost?" he asked.

Baxfield held the watch in his trembling hand and replied hesitatingly, "I believe it is, but I won't swear to it."

There was a pause. Then, in grave, impressive tones, Thorndyke said," Now, Mr. Baxfield, I am going to ask you a question which you need not answer if you consider that by doing so you would prejudice your position in any way. That question is, When your pocket was picked, were any articles besides this watch taken from your person? Don't hurry. Consider your answer carefully."

For some moments Baxfield remained silent, regarding Thorndyke with a wild, affrighted stare. At length he began falteringly, "I don't remember missing any thing–" and then stopped.

"Could the witness be allowed to sit down, sir?" Thorndyke asked. And when the permission had been given and a chair placed, Baxfield sat down heavily and cast a bewildered glance round the court. "I think," he said, addressing Thorndyke, "I had better tell you exactly what happened and take my chance of the consequences. When I left my uncle's house on Monday, I took a circuit through the fields and then entered Gilbert's Copse to wait for my uncle and tell him what I thought of his conduct in leaving the bulk of his property to a stranger. I struck the path that I knew my uncle would take and walked along it slowly to meet him. I did meet him – on the path, just above where he was found – and I began to say what was in my mind. But he wouldn't listen. He flew into a rage, and as I was standing in the middle of the path, he tried to push past me. In doing so he caught his foot in a bramble and staggered back, then he disappeared through the bushes and a few seconds after I heard a thud down below. I pulled the bushes aside and looked down into the chalk-pit, and there I saw him lying with his head all on one side. Now, I happened to know of a short cut down into the pit. It was rather a dangerous climb, but I took it to get down as quickly as possible. It was there that I dropped the cigarette-tube. When I got to my uncle I could see that he was dead. His skull was battered and his neck was broken. Then the devil put into my head the idea of making away with the will. But I knew that if I took the will only, suspicion would fall on me. So I took most of his valuables – the wallet, his watch and chain, his purse and his ring. The purse I emptied and threw away, and flung the ring after it. I took the will out of the wallet – it had just been dropped in loose – and put it in an inner pocket. Then I dropped the wallet and the watch and chain into my outside coat pocket.

"I struck across country, intending to make for the race-course and drop the things among the crowd, so that they might be picked up and safely carried away. But when I got there a gang of pickpockets saved me the trouble; they mobbed and hustled me and cleared my pockets of everything but my keys and the will."

"And what has become of the will?" asked Thorndyke.

"I have it here." He dipped into his breast pocket and produced a folded paper, which he handed to Thorndyke, who opened it, and having glanced at it, passed it to the coroner.

That was practically the end of the inquest. The jury decided to accept Baxfield's statement and recorded a verdict of "Death by Misadventure," leaving Baxfield to be dealt with by the proper authorities.

"An interesting and eminently satisfactory case," remarked Thorndyke, as we sat over a rather late dinner. "Essentially simple, too. The elucidation turned, as you probably noticed, on a single illuminating fact."

"I judged that it was so," said I, "though the illumination of that fact has not yet reached me."

"Well," said Thorndyke, "let us first take the general aspect of the case as it was presented by Marchmont. The first thing, of course, that struck one was that the loss of the will might easily have converted Baxfield from a minor beneficiary to the sole heir. But even if the court agreed to recognise the will, it would have to be guided by the statements of the only two men to whom its provisions were even approximately known, and Baxfield could have made any statement he pleased. It was impossible to ignore the fact that the loss of the will was very greatly to Baxfield's advantage.

"When the stolen property was discovered in Fletcher's possession it looked, at the first glance, as if the mystery of the crime were solved. But there were several serious inconsistencies. First, how came Fletcher to be in this solitary wood, remote from any railway or even road? He appeared to be a London pickpocket. When he was killed he was travelling to London by train. It seemed probable that he had come from London by train to ply his trade at the races. Then, as you know, criminological experience shows that the habitual criminal is a rigid specialist. The burglar, the coiner, the pickpocket, each keeps strictly to his own special line Now, Fletcher was a pickpocket, and had evidently be picking pockets on the race-course. The probabilities were against his being the original robber and in favour of his having picked the pocket of the person who robbed Harewood. But if this were so, who was that person? Once more the probabilities suggested Baxfield. There was the motive, as I have said, and further, the pocket-picking had apparently taken place on the race-course, and Baxfield was known to be a frequenter of race-courses. But again, if Baxfield were the person robbed by Fletcher, then one of the five watches was probably Baxfield's watch. Whether it was so or not might have been very difficult to prove, but here came in the single illuminating fact that I have spoken of.

"You remember that when Marchmont opened the case he mentioned that Baxfield was a manufacturer of felt hats, and Crowhurst told us that he was a sort of foreman or manager of the factory."

"Yes, I remember, now you speak of it. But what is the bearing of the fact?"

"My dear Jervis!" exclaimed Thorndyke. "Don't you see that it gave us a touchstone? Consider, now. What is a felt hat? It is just a mass of agglutinated rabbits' hair. The process of manufacture consists in blowing a jet of the more or less disintegrated hair on to a revolving steel cone which is moistened by a spray of an alcoholic solution of shellac. But, of course, a quantity of the finer and more minute particles of the broken hairs miss the cone and float about in the air. The air of the factory is thus charged with the dust of broken rabbit hairs; and this dust settles on and penetrates the clothing of the workers. But when clothing becomes charged with dust, that dust tends to accumulate in the pockets and find its way into the hollows and interstices of any object carried in those pockets. Thus, if one of the five watches was Baxfield's it would almost certainly show traces where this characteristic dust had crept under the bezel and settled on the dial. And so it turned out to be. When I inspected those five watches through the Coddington lens, on the dial of No. 3 I saw a quantity of dust of this character. The electrified vulcanite rod picked it all up neatly and transferred it to the slide, and under the microscope its nature was obvious. The owner of this watch was therefore, almost certainly, employed in a felt hat factory. But, of course, it was necessary to show not only the presence of rabbit hair in this watch but its absence in the others and in Fletcher's pockets; which I did.

"Then with regard to Harewood's watch. There was no rabbit hair on the dial, but there was a small quantity on the fluff from the key barrel. Now, if that rabbit hair had come from Harewood's pocket it would have been uniformly distributed through the fluff. But it was not. It was confined exclusively to the part of the fluff that was exposed. Thus it had come from some pocket other than Harewood's and the owner of that pocket was almost certainly employed in a felt hat factory, and was most probably the owner of watch No. 3. Then there was the cigarette-tube. Its bore was loaded with rabbit hair. But its owner had unquestionably been at the scene of the crime. There was a clear suggestion that his was the pocket in which the stolen watch had been carried and that he was the owner of watch No. 3. The problem was to piece this evidence together and prove definitely who this person was. And that I was able to do by means of a fresh item of evidence, which I acquired when I saw Baxfield at the inquest. I suppose you noticed his boots?"

"I am afraid I didn't," I had to admit.

"Well, I did. I watched his feet constantly, and when he crossed his legs I could see that he had iron toe-tips on his boots. That was what gave me confidence to push the cross-examination."

"It was certainly a rather daring cross-examination and rather irregular, too," said I.

It was extremely irregular," Thorndyke agreed. "The coroner ought not to have permitted it. But it was all for the best. If the coroner had disallowed my questions we should have had to take criminal proceedings against Baxfield, whereas now that we have recovered the will, it is possible that no one will trouble to prosecute him."

Which, I subsequently ascertained, is what actually happened.

TO LOVE
AND
BE WISE

Josephine Tey

AN INSPECTOR GRANT MYSTERY

This is the sixth of Josephine Tey's 'Inspector Grant' novels from the golden age of British detective fiction. Grant meets a celebrity photographer, Leslie Searle, briefly at a party in London. He is later astonished to hear that he has vanished in the sleepy village of Salcott St. Mary and sets off to investigate.

Hardcover 2010, Oxford City Press
ISBN-10: **1849025991**, ISBN-13: **978-1-84902-599-7**